THE TRAP WAS SPRUNG. . . .

"You can't take us in for tryin' to steal some rocks," Arch said.

"I can take you in for a lot of other things you've done, Dolan," replied the Gunsmith. "Once you're in custody we can work on bringing your father in."

"Forget that. You'll never catch that old man. He don't even leave home no more."

"He will when we have you," Clint said. "Come on, drop 'em."

Arch and Harvey exchanged a glance but before they could act a scream ripped through the air, and then Sammy Dolan was riding into camp, his gun drawn.

"Come on, Arch!" he shouted, firing at Clint. The shot missed, and Clint didn't give him another chance. He drew and fired.

THE LAST BOUNTY

J. R. ROBERTS

JOVE BOOKS, NEW YORK

THE LAST BOUNTY

A Jove Book / published by arrangement with
the author

PRINTING HISTORY
Jove edition / May 1999

The Penguin Putnam Inc. World Wide Web site address is
http://www.penguinputnam.com

ISBN: 0-515-12512-1

A JOVE BOOK®
Jove Books are published by The Berkley Publishing Group,
a division of Penguin Putnam Inc.,
375 Hudson Street, New York, New York 10014.
JOVE and the "J" design
are trademarks belonging to Penguin Putnam Inc.

PRINTED IN THE UNITED STATES OF AMERICA

10 9 8 7 6 5 4 3 2 1

THE GUNSMITH

208

THE LAST BOUNTY

ONE

Kate Martin was as energetic a woman as Clint Adams had ever been in bed with. She was tall, blond, willowy, with breasts the shape and firmness of peaches just before they start to get ripe. They had met the very first day he arrived in Prescott, Oregon, and had spent each of the next three nights together. She'd hurriedly informed him that she didn't usually do this, but hadn't he felt the spark between them when he first entered the store?

He had indeed felt something the first time he saw her behind the counter of Martin's Mercantile. The store belonged to her father, but she'd been working the counter that day. She was wearing a simple cotton dress that buttoned at her neck and molded itself to her breasts, which he noticed and made the connection to peaches right away. He couldn't imagine that they were as firm as they appeared to be.

He found out that first night, when she knocked on his hotel room door and told him about the "spark."

"You don't have to worry," she'd said, seating herself on his bed. "I don't expect you to fall in love with me and sweep me away from here. In fact, I quite like it here.

1

I just don't believe we should waste any time, do you?''

Her eyes were blue and very bright at that moment and he'd said, ''No, we shouldn't.''

She'd nearly worn him out that first night. He was getting to the age where he should probably be leaving women in their early to mid-twenties alone, but Kate simply wouldn't *let* him do that. She was insistent and he was weak—at least, that was what he told himself. When she peeled off her dress, discarded her underwear, and stood up, his palms immediately began to itch . . . an itch that was only eased when he put his hands over her breasts and felt them.

''Peaches,'' she said.

''Perfect,'' he said, and they went to bed.

Now it was the morning of the fourth day. The fatigue was present in his legs again, as Kate had insisted on waking him in the middle of the night so they could ''do it'' a third time. He didn't know if he'd ever heard a woman use the phrase ''do it'' before when referring to having sex. Maybe it was something the younger folks were using. However, the warmth of her breath in his ear and the smoothness and heat of her body pressed against his had definitely put his body in the mood to ''do it.''

He had come to Prescott to meet up with a friend of his—an old friend named Amos Weatherby. If Weatherby didn't arrive soon, though, trying to keep up with Kate Martin might end up killing him!

For instance, here it was barely first light and she was pressed against him again.

''Kate—''

''Clint,'' she said, lifting one leg over him, ''I can't sleep.''

''I can.''

"No, no," she said, sliding onto him so that he could feel that wiry, curly hair between her legs rubbing against him. "No, you can't."

Suddenly, she was rubbing her furry patch up and down the length of his penis. In moments he could feel her wetness and himself getting hard.

"Jesus," he said, "I don't know how you do it, girl."

"Do what?"

"Get me ready every time."

She laughed, lifted her hips, reached between them to grasp him, and then sat down on him, taking him inside of her.

"You want it as much as I do," she whispered. "That's the secret."

She leaned over so he could kiss her breasts and bite her nipples while she rode him up and down. It drove her crazy when he did that—but then everything seemed to drive her crazy. In minutes she was bouncing up and down on him with abandon, her breath coming in gasps and grunts. Once she bounced up so violently that he popped out of her. She grabbed his slick penis, stuffed it back inside of her, and found her rhythm again with no trouble.

Her insides were like velvet, and she tugged at him, as if she were grasping him every time she came down on him and pulling on him when she bounced up. He swore sometimes it felt almost like a *hand* was tugging on him, or as if she were sucking him with her wet mouth— which, by the way, she did wonderfully, driving *him* crazy.

In this instance, however, Kate Martin was concerned with only one thing: her own pleasure. That was all right with Clint, though. It excited him to see her like this, her eyes closed, biting her lip, losing control as she bounced up and down on him, seeking her pleasure, rushing toward it and then going wild as it took hold of her, and wilder still when he finally exploded inside of her. . . .

TWO

Amos Weatherby was a legend to some people. Not the people who thought of Wild Bill Hickok as a legend, or Wyatt Earp, or Bat Masterson, or Clint Adams. No, the people who thought of Weatherby as a legend were the people *other* thought of as legends: Hickok, Earp, Masterson, and especially Clint Adams.

Weatherby had been a lawman in the West when the West was truly untamed. Toward the end of his career, when he gave up wearing a badge, he had turned to bounty hunting. The money, however, was secondary. Amos Weatherby was still doing what he felt he had been born to do: bring bad men to justice.

Clint had met Weatherby as a very young man and had learned a lot. He hadn't learned how to use a gun; that came naturally. What Clint had learned, however, was when to use it and, more importantly, when *not* to use it. Even during his brief career as a bounty hunter, Weatherby had brought most of his prey back alive. Clint had learned other things, too. How to relate to people and even more so, to women. Amos Weatherby had always been a ladies' man.

Clint was in Prescott, Oregon, to see Amos Weatherby, and he wondered why. After all, Weatherby had been retired as a manhunter for a few years now and had recently turned seventy years old. And the telegram Clint had received through Rick Hartman in Labyrinth, Texas, had said only that Weatherby "needed his help." He could only hope that his old friend hadn't gotten himself deeply into trouble, but couldn't imagine what other reason there could be for the summons.

He could only wait and see.

On the morning of that fourth day, Clint left Kate up in his room and went down for breakfast. Kate stayed willowy by never eating breakfast, but being with her all night built up an appetite in Clint that he couldn't deny. After his hunger for Kate had been quenched, he needed to go down and have breakfast. She usually spent several more hours in his bed before dressing and going to work. Clint didn't know if she went back home to change, and if she did he didn't know what she told her mother and father, with whom she still lived. That was her business and he didn't pry. It was enough for him that she wanted to spend the nights with him.

"When is your friend arriving?" she'd asked that morning.

"According to his telegram," Clint said, while he dressed, "two days ago."

"Well, we've had two extra days, then," she said, "but it could all end at any time."

He looked at her and said, "Just because he gets here— whenever he gets here—doesn't necessarily mean I'll be leaving right away."

"That's true, it doesn't."

"At least," he said, on his way to the door, "not without saying good-bye."

As he pulled the door closed he heard something strike it from the other side, then heard her laugh.

He chuckled now, while waiting for his food, thinking of that infectious, bawdy laugh of hers—probably the best laugh he'd ever heard on a woman.

The waiter, Tom, had served Clint every morning, and he knew what to bring as soon as he saw him.

"Your steak and eggs, Mr. Adams," Tom said, setting the plate down in front of him.

"Thanks, Tom."

"Your friend hasn't arrived yet, eh?"

"No."

Everyone knew Clint was waiting for someone. Even the desk clerk had greeted him that morning in the lobby with, "No sign of him yet, huh?"

"I can use another pot of coffee, Tom," Clint said.

"Comin' up, sir."

He tucked into his steak and eggs, once again thinking about Amos Weatherby. The last telegram he'd received from him had been about three years ago, when Weatherby announced he was retiring. Clint had no idea what the man had been doing since then. That was something they could talk about, when he finally got there.

And what was he supposed to do if Weatherby didn't show up? Assume he'd changed his mind? Or that whatever trouble had prompted his request for help had caught up with him? Where would he begin to look?

Well, the logical place would be Willowridge, the town near Seattle where Weatherby had sent the telegram from. Seattle wasn't so far from Prescott, which was just east of Portland, that it would take Weatherby this long to get there. Certainly, he should have gotten there ahead of Clint.

Clint decided to give Amos Weatherby a week. If he hadn't arrived by then, Clint was just going to have to go and find him.

THREE

There was no need for Clint to go looking for Amos Weatherby, though, because later that day, while he was lounging in a chair in front of his hotel, Weatherby came riding down the street. Seventy years old and he sat his horse as ramrod straight as he had ten, twenty, or thirty years ago.

Clint did notice, however, how thin Weatherby was. As the man came closer Clint saw the gaunt hollows in the man's cheeks and the look on his face. Weatherby may have been sitting in his saddle straight as he ever had, but the man was definitely in pain.

Weatherby rode right up to the hotel and looked down at Clint.

"I'd dismount and shake your hand, son," he said, "but then I'd have to get right back up here and ride this sucker to the nearest livery, and I don't think I'll be able to do that."

Clint stepped down into the street and reached up to shake his old friend's hand. The grip was as firm as ever, but Weatherby's skin was as dry as paper.

"What's going on, Amos?"

"This where you're stayin'?" Weatherby asked, looking up at the hotel.

"That's right."

"Let me get my horse taken care of, then I'll come over and get a room. After that we can have a talk. Okay?"

"Whatever you say, Amos," Clint replied. "You're calling the shots here."

"Don't you worry none, Clint," Weatherby said. "This trip is gonna be worth your while. I guarantee it."

Clint watched Weatherby ride the rest of the way down the street. He'd been able to see the pain in his friend's eyes, and now he could see it in the way he rode.

Something was very wrong with Amos Weatherby.

Clint waited in front of the hotel until he saw Weatherby walking back up the street. The man's steps seemed to be very deliberate. He was carrying his rifle in one hand and his saddlebags were slung over one bony shoulder. Clint noticed he wasn't wearing a gun. Now that Weatherby was down from his horse, Clint had the impression that he had gotten shorter, but he figured that would happen to everyone, eventually.

As Weatherby reached him the two men shook hands again.

"Let me get checked in and then we'll get a drink," Weatherby said. "We have a lot to talk about."

"All right."

Clint stood by while the older man got a room, and flashed back to times as a young man when he would stand by and wait for Amos Weatherby to finish what he was doing so he could talk to him. He'd learned a lot just listening to the man.

"Can you have someone take my gear to my room?" Weatherby asked the desk clerk.

"Certainly, sir."

Weatherby looked at Clint and said, "The old legs ain't what they used to be. When I go up them steps I aim to stay a while."

"I know how you feel."

"No," Weatherby said, "you don't. Come on, let's go and get that drink."

They walked together to the saloon, and for a man who seemed to have a lot to say Weatherby was quiet the whole way. It wasn't until they had each settled in at a back table in the mostly empty saloon with a beer that the man started to talk.

"I'm dyin', Clint."

"What?"

"It's true," Weatherby said. "A doctor in San Francisco says there's somethin' eatin' my insides. A cancer, he called it."

Clint took no satisfaction in the fact that he'd been right about the pain in Weatherby's eyes.

"Well, can't they do something?"

"No," Weatherby said. "He gave me somethin' for the pain but he says even that won't help me much in a month or so."

"A month?"

"Maybe more, maybe less."

"Jesus, Amos, I'm sorry."

"Don't be," Weatherby said. "I'm seventy, I've lasted longer in the manhunter game than most men."

"Yeah, I guess you have."

"But there's one last thing I've got to do before I die."

"And what's that?"

"I've got to bring in Chance Dolan and his boys."

"His boys?"

"Sons," Weatherby said. "Old Chance has got his sons workin' with him now."

Chance Dolan was the one man who had eluded Weatherby all these years.

"Amos, isn't Chance, uh, about your age, now?" Clint asked.

"Same age, I reckon," Weatherby replied. "Clint, I can't die and leave that old bandit out there."

"How do you expect to bring him in? Especially if he's got his sons with him?"

"I'm gonna have some help, too."

"Who?"

Weatherby smiled.

FOUR

"Now, wait a minute, Amos."

"Who else would I rather have backin' me up?" Weatherby asked.

"I'm not a bounty hunter."

"Well, neither am I, anymore. Besides, you know I never really did it for the bounty."

"I know."

"So when we bring them in," Weatherby said, "we'll donate the money to some church, or something. I just have to do this before I die, Clint."

"Wait a minute."

"What is it?"

Clint eyed Weatherby suspiciously. "Is this on the level, Amos?"

"Clint!" Weatherby protested. "I'm shocked that you'd think I'd lie to you about somethin' like this. Have I ever lied to you before?"

"How about that time in Tucson? You told me that girl was interested in me."

"Well, she was. If I remember correctly, you spent a nice afternoon with her."

"Yeah, until her boyfriend came walking in," Clint pointed out. "You didn't tell me that she was waiting for her boyfriend with the bounty on his head to show up."

"I told you then," Weatherby said, "it slipped my mind."

"Yeah, well, what about Denver—"

"Hey, everybody lies in Denver."

"Amos—"

"Look, Clint," Weatherby said, "I'll give you the name of my doctor if you want; you can send him a telegram. He'll confirm what I'm tellin' you."

Clint studied his old friend and sometime mentor for a few moments, then said, "Never mind. I don't have to check. I'll take your word for it. Besides, you don't look so good."

"It shows, huh?"

"In the way you walk, and sit your horse. And that's another thing."

"What?"

"How are you going to track Chance and his sons?"

"I'll just have to, that's all," Weatherby said. "I ain't lettin' him get away scot-free."

"How many sons does he have, anyway?"

"I don't really know," Weatherby said, "two or three . . ."

"Or more?"

"Naw, I don't think . . . well, maybe four. I'm not sure. But you and I can handle 'em, Clint. Just like the old days."

"It's not the old days, Amos."

Weatherby shifted uncomfortably in his chair and said, "Boy, don't I know it. My butt is sore. Listen, I got to go to my room and lie down for a while."

"And take your pain medicine?"

"Er, yeah, I could use some of that."

"All right," Clint said. "We'll continue this later."

"Continue what?"

"You can keep trying to convince me to help you later," Clint said.

"You mean you ain't convinced? You ain't gonna do it?" Weatherby asked.

"I don't know yet, Amos," Clint said. "I'll have to think about it."

"Clint," Weatherby said, getting painfully to his feet, "you ain't about to turn down a dyin' man's last wish, are you?"

"You may be dying," Clint said, "but you haven't changed a bit, have you? You can still use guilt to get your way."

"Well, let's face it," Weatherby said. "Guilt is a good weapon this time, and the only one I've got."

"What about friendship?"

"Would you do it if I asked you to, just in the name of friendship?"

Clint thought a moment, then said, "Yeah, I think, I would."

"Well, okay, then. I'll ask in the name of—"

"Later," Clint broke in. "Ask me again later." He stood up. "Right now let's get you back to the hotel."

"Okay," Weatherby said, "but we got to walk slowly, okay?"

"Sure."

As they walked back to the hotel—slowly—Clint tried to figure out how Weatherby expected to track Chance Dolan and his sons on horseback if he could hardly put one foot in front of the other.

And after years and years of trying to bring Dolan to justice, what made Amos Weatherby so sure now he could do it in a month's time—or less?

FIVE

Once he left Weatherby in his room Clint wished he had asked for the name of his friend's doctor, not so much to check his story as to simply check his condition and ask some questions.

Clint left the hotel, went to the telegraph office, and sent a wire to Rick Hartman asking if he'd heard anything about Weatherby's condition. He also asked for some doctors' names in San Francisco who might know something about cancer.

He arranged for the reply to be brought to the hotel and, in his absence, left with the desk clerk. He then went to the hotel and told the desk clerk he was waiting for a telegram. He asked the man to hold it for him if it came in, and not to tell anyone about it.

Once all of that was done, he didn't know quite what to do next. He and Weatherby still had some talking to do when the older man felt up to it, so the only thing Clint could do was wait for him to wake up, hopefully feeling better.

He left the hotel and walked over to Martin's Mercantile. Kate smiled at him when he entered. Her father was stocking some shelves, but when Clint entered he gave him a dirty look and went into the back room.

"Let me guess," Clint said. "He knows about us."

"He confronted me about it when I got home today, so I told him."

"Told him what, exactly?"

"That we're friends," she said, and then added, "close friends."

"What did he say to that?"

"He asked if you were going to marry me."

"And?"

"And I told him that was a silly question, that we hardly knew each other."

Clint could just imagine what her father had said to that. She knew a man well enough to sleep with him, but not to marry him?

"Never mind him," she said. "Did your friend get here today?"

"Yes, he did."

"Well," she said, "I don't know whether to be happy about that or not."

"Save your decision until I tell you a story," Clint said, and told her about Weatherby's illness.

"Oh, Clint," she said, covering his hand with hers, "I'm so sorry."

"I know. I am, too."

"But how does he expect to track these men down when he's dying?"

"If he has his way he'll die in the saddle," Clint said, "and not in some hotel bed."

"And will you help him to die in the saddle?" she asked.

"I don't know what else I can do, Kate. We still have some talking to do, but I'm sure of one thing."

"What's that?"

"If I don't help him," Clint said, "he'll try it alone."

"Maybe that's what he wants," she said.

"What?"

"Maybe he doesn't want to die in the saddle—maybe he wants to die in a hail of bullets. That would add to his legend, wouldn't it? And keep him from dying slowly over the next month or so?"

"You might have a point."

"And how would you feel if you help him to die that way?"

He knew she was intimating that he'd feel guilty, but her attempts to dissuade him had just the opposite effect.

"Actually," he said, "I'd feel pretty damn good about it."

"What?"

"Well, that's the way *I'd* rather go. I wouldn't want to die slowly of some disease that was eating me away from the inside out."

She made a face, but said nothing.

"I hope if that happens that someone would help me die a better way."

He thought briefly of Doc Holliday, who for years had been getting eaten away from the inside out, coughing up bloody bits of his lungs into handkerchiefs. There would be none of that for him and none of it for Amos Weatherby, either.

He leaned over and kissed Kate on the cheek.

"Thanks, Kate," he said. "You helped me make up my mind."

"Not the way I was trying to, though."

"Maybe not," he said, "but it's the right way. I'll see you later?"

"Will you?"

"Oh, yes," he promised. "We won't be leaving for a

day or two. Besides, I meant what I said this morning.''

''What was that?''

''I wouldn't leave without saying good-bye to you,'' he reminded her.

''I'm going to hold you to that, Clint Adams,'' she called as he went out the door.

SIX

When Clint got back to the hotel he knocked on Weatherby's door. When there was no answer he decided to check the dining room. If his friend wasn't there he was going to have to get a key to his room and check on him. He dreaded the thought of finding Weatherby dead or dying in a hotel bed, which only strengthened his resolve to help Weatherby end his life the way he wanted to—on a horse, with a gun in his hand.

He breathed a sigh of relief when he found Weatherby in the dining room having a cup of coffee and a piece of pie.

"There you are," he said, dropping into the chair opposite him.

"Had you worried?" Weatherby asked. "Thought I was dead already?"

"The thought had crossed my mind."

"Not likely," the old manhunter said. "I'm not going until I put ol' Chance behind bars—or six feet under before me."

"And his boys?"

"The posters say dead or alive on all three of them,"

Weatherby said. "With me it's always been their choice, Clint, you know that."

"I know that, Amos," Clint said. "There's still posters out on Chance?"

"Yep, and his boys have joined him. Now the whole family is wanted."

"Where?"

"Half a dozen states."

"Where are they now?"

"Goddamn pie," Weatherby said, putting his fork down. "It's all I can keep down these—you mean you're gonna help me?"

"If you still want me to."

"That's great!" Weatherby exclaimed, reaching out to pump Clint's hand. "It'll be like old times."

"I hope not," Clint said. "I remember some of those old times as being pretty dangerous."

"Ah," Weatherby said, "Chance is an old man now. He won't be so hard to catch."

"What about his boys?"

"Too inexperienced to give us any trouble. Together we'll just be too much for them, Clint."

"I hope you're right. So tell me, Amos, where are they?"

"Well," Weatherby said, "they're in one of two places. Missouri or Oklahoma."

"I think we have to narrow it down a little more than that."

"Well, they live in Missouri," Weatherby said, "but they been raising hell in Oklahoma."

"Do you know exactly where they live?"

"Not really," Weatherby said. "See, Chance is sort of well-thought-of by his neighbors in Missouri, the way Frank and Jesse were."

"You mean they hide him out?"

"Pretty much. I think we're gonna have to catch them in the act."

"In Oklahoma."

"Right."

"How will we know when and where they're going to strike?"

"I've been thinkin' about that," Weatherby said. "I think what we're gonna have to do is set a trap for 'em."

"And how do we do that?"

"We come up with something they just won't be able to resist."

"Like what?"

Weatherby sat back and shifted uncomfortably.

"I haven't exactly figured that out yet."

"Well, then," Clint said, "we'd better get another pot of coffee if you expect me to be of any help."

Clint signaled Tom the waiter and pointed at the coffeepot. Tom nodded and went to get another.

"You got that boy trained."

"Well, I've been here a few days," Clint said pointedly. "You were late, you know."

"Yeah, I know," Weatherby said. "Couldn't be helped. I don't travel as well as I used to."

"So how do you expect to get from here to Oklahoma?"

"Train. Once we're there we can tie me to my horse if we have to."

That prospect didn't thrill Clint much.

"Amos, are you sure you're going to be up to this?"

"The truth?"

"The truth," Clint said, nodding.

"I ain't sure, Clint," Weatherby said. "I ain't sure at all. I wanna do this, I know that. What's that they say about the mind bein' willin' but the flesh weak? That really is what the problem is. But I tell you one thing. I got a helluva better chance of gettin' it done with you than without you.''

"Well," Clint said, "you don't have to worry about that, Amos. I'm in for the long haul."

"Well, lucky for you the long haul don't look so all-fired long, this time," Weatherby said.

Somehow, Clint didn't think that was funny.

SEVEN

They decided that Weatherby should get a full day's rest—meaning that Clint decided they'd leave after his friend had two good nights' sleep in a bed.

"A day's rest," Weatherby complained. "That means today."

"A full day's rest, I said," Clint said. "You got here today, tomorrow will be a full day's rest. We'll leave day after tomorrow."

They decided to ride to the nearest railhead and take the train to Kansas City. From there they would continue on horseback—as soon as they knew where to continue to.

Their plan was to plant a story in Kansas and Missouri newspapers about a gold shipment, the size of which Chance Dolan and his sons would not be able to resist. They each knew enough people in the newspaper business to get this done without much problem.

This would serve to bring the Dolan gang to them, which would make it unnecessary for Weatherby to sit a horse while they tracked them.

Weatherby went right from the dining room to his room to begin his rest.

"I'll rest," he said, "but I doubt I'll sleep. I don't sleep so good, these days."

"Can I get you anything, Amos?"

"Well, yeah, as a matter of fact, you can," Weatherby said. "You could bring me a woman."

"What? In your condition you want a woman?"

"I'm glad you didn't say at my age," Weatherby commented dryly.

"I wouldn't say that," Clint said. "I hope when I'm your age I still want a woman, but—"

"Relax, Clint. I always sleep better with a warm woman in bed with me. Maybe, with a woman, I might get some sleep."

"Are you serious?"

"Very."

Clint gave in. "Well, all right. I'll bring you a woman."

"And I don't care if I have to pay," Weatherby said. "I don't have that same rule you do, you know, about payin' for a woman."

"I know."

"In fact, I'd prefer to pay," the older man said. "That way she'll do a good job."

"I thought you just wanted to sleep!"

"I'm talkin' in general," Weatherby said. "I always liked it when a woman thought she had to earn her money. She always made sure I was happy, then."

Clint had never thought of it that way. He'd always wanted a woman to come to his bed willingly. The way Weatherby explained it, paying wasn't so bad—but he wasn't about to change his way of doing things now.

"You go to your room, and I'll see what I can do," he said.

"Thanks. I knew I could count on you."

Clint started to watch Weatherby climb the stairs to the second floor but it was too painful, so he turned and left the hotel.

Clint thought about asking Kate if she knew any women who wouldn't mind sleeping with a seventy-year-old man, but then dismissed that as being silly. Instead, he went to the saloon to talk to the bartender.

"Ned, I need a woman," he said.

Ned, in his forties and overweight, said, "So do I, Clint."

"No, you don't understand," Clint replied. "It's not for me, it's for a friend."

"Are you trying to set him up with a date, or are you pimping now?"

At the word "pimp," Clint winced. "It's not like that," he said. "I have a friend who just needs some company."

"Company?"

"Yeah."

"For the night? That kind of company?"

"Well . . . yeah, sort of."

"What does 'sort of' mean?"

"He's sick," Clint began. "He can't really, uh, do anything with a woman, but he likes to sleep with them."

"You mean really sleep?"

"Right."

"Well, I'm sure one of the girls here would be available for the right price."

"Your girls are all kind of . . . young."

"What's that got to do with anything?"

"My friend is, uh, seventy."

"Seventy years old?"

"Yes."

"Wow, no wonder he just wants to sleep with a girl."

"A woman," Clint said. "He wants to sleep with a woman."

"Well, if all he wants to do is sleep, Clint, why is age a problem?" Ned wanted to know.

Clint thought that over for a moment, then replied, "I guess you're right."

"Why don't you talk to the girls when they come to work and see what they say?"

"Okay, I will."

"Maybe they'll even believe you that your friend just wants to *sleep* with them—really sleep."

"It's the truth."

"Hey," Ned said, "*I* believe you. . . ."

EIGHT

"You what?"

"I found him a woman."

Kate sat up in bed and stared down at Clint. The sheet fell away from her, revealing her peach tits in all their glory.

"That's the same as being a pimp."

"No, it's not," Clint said. "He's my friend—"

"How could you do that to that old man?" she broke in. "And what about the girl? What's she going to expect when she goes into that room?"

"She's been in there for a while," he said, "and I haven't heard any complaints."

"Wha—How old is she?" Kate demanded.

"I didn't want to get him someone *too* young," he explained. "She's twenty-nine."

"Twenty-nine?" she repeated. "And he's seventy? She'll give him a heart attack, Clint."

He laughed and said, "No, she won't, Kate. They're not going to do anything but sleep."

"Does she know that?"

"Yes, she does. I made it clear to her that all she was

going to have to do was share a bed—and her warmth.''

"And she was okay with that?''

"Yes.''

"Is she—I mean, is she a prostitute?''

"She's a saloon girl.''

"Isn't that the same thing?''

"No, it's not. Lie back down here and stop looking at me so disapprovingly.''

She hesitated, then did as he asked. He covered her with the sheet and put his arm around her, and she snuggled closer.

"I guess it's all right,'' she said. "I mean, he is dying, isn't he?''

"Yes, he is.''

"So this is like a last wish?''

"Well, almost,'' Clint said. "He's got something else he wants to do before he dies.''

"Oh, that's right,'' she said. "One last bounty, and you're going to help him with that, too.''

"Yes, I am,'' he said. "He's probably my oldest friend. Hell, over the years he's been a friend *and* a mentor. I can't just let him do this by himself. What kind of a person would I be if I turned my back on a friend when he was dying?''

"Not a very good one, I suppose.''

"That's an understatement.''

"I'm sorry,'' she said, snuggling closer. "I don't have any right to judge what you do.''

She was right about that, but Clint remained quiet.

"When will you be leaving?'' she asked.

"Day after tomorrow.''

"So that gives us one more night after tonight.''

"Right.''

"Well,'' she said, sliding her hand down his body, "I

guess we might as well make the most of it.''

As she took hold of him Clint knew that meant he wasn't going to be getting much sleep this night.

Down the hall Amos Weatherby stirred, was confused for a moment, then realized there was a woman in bed with him. Her name was Lila. When she'd arrived at his room she smiled at him and said, ''You're cute.''

''And harmless,'' he said. ''Were you told about my . . . situation?''

''I was told you wanted a warm body to sleep with,'' she said. ''That's all.''

''Right.''

She shucked her dress with practiced ease, and he took in the sight of her naked body. She was a big woman, with full breasts and hips, and he knew when she turned around he'd seen a fine, big butt. Clint had done well, sending him a real woman and not a girl who was more bones than skin.

''Which side of the bed d'ya want?'' she asked.

He had given her the choice, and she'd picked the right side. They'd gotten into bed together—she naked, he with his union suit—and she had pressed herself close to him, plastering the length of her full, warm body to his.

''Is this okay?''

''This is fine,'' he said.

They had fallen asleep, but now he was awake and trying to figure out what had awakened him. Suddenly, he realized what it was. In her sleep she had somehow slipped her hand inside his long underwear—and he had an erection! A fine, big, hard, throbbing erection like he hadn't had in some time. The doctor had warned him that his illness would affect his performance with a woman, but he had reminded the doctor that he was seventy years old, so that probably wouldn't be a problem. The doctor retorted that *he* was seventy-five and he and his wife still had relations, adding if he couldn't do that he'd rather be dead.

Lila's hand was on his chest, but now she moaned and slid her hand down. He didn't know what she was dreaming about but before he knew it her hand was down between his legs, holding on to him.

And then she was awake.

"Oh, my," she said.

"Sorry."

But she didn't let go. Instead she stroked his penis gently, running her fingertips up and down the underside, making him groan.

"How long's it been for you?" she asked.

"A long time," he said, "and I didn't think ever again."

"Be a shame to waste this," she said, still stroking.

"It wasn't part of the bargain, ma'am," he said. "I didn't think I'd be able—"

"Shhh," she whispered, increasing the pressure of her strokes now. "Let's just say it's on the house, okay?"

"Jeez—" He closed his eyes, then, giving himself up to the sensations her hand was causing.

"Let's get these open," she said, undoing the buttons of his underwear. Suddenly, his hard penis was out in the open. "Ah!"

And then he was in her mouth, and it was the most amazing thing that had happened to him in a long, long, time. . . .

NINE

As Clint left his hotel room the next morning, quietly closing the door behind him so as not to awaken Kate, the door to Weatherby's room opened and Lila stepped out, also trying to be quiet.

They turned and saw each other and Lila smiled. Clint felt awkward.

Lila came sashaying up to him, put her hands on her hips, and said, "I thought you said your friend was a dying man."

"He is."

"Well," she said, "he sure didn't act like it last night—or maybe little Lila just has the power to raise the dead, huh?"

She gave her lips a lascivious lick, then turned and walked down the hall to the stairs, twitching her hips as she went.

"What the hell . . . ?" was all Clint could say. He almost knocked on Weatherby's door to ask him what had happened last night, but he decided against it. Whatever had gone on between him and Lila, Clint had no doubt that he was a sick man. He decided just to go down and eat and wait for his friend to wake up on his own.

Tom brought him his usual breakfast and asked, "Will your friend be joining you, Mr. Adams?"

"I'm not sure, Tom," Clint said. "We'll just have to wait and see."

Tom didn't leave.

"Is there something you need?" Clint asked.

"I know who he is, you know."

"Who?"

"Amos Weatherby. Not a lot of people remember him anymore, but I do."

"Why's that?"

"I was in Wichita twenty years ago when he brought in the Harvey Brothers. The newspapers said he was fifty then. Can that be true? Is he seventy now?"

"I'm afraid he is."

Tom shook his head and said, "In my opinion he should be as famous as Hickok or . . . or . . . well, you."

"I'll tell him you think so."

"I just had to say something, you know?"

"Sure."

"Let me know if you need anything else."

"I will."

The waiter went away and Clint concentrated on his breakfast.

When Weatherby didn't show up by the time he finished eating, Clint was worried enough to go up to his room and knock on the door. He had to knock three times and was about to go down to the desk for a key when he heard Weatherby call out, "Come in."

When he opened the door and entered he saw Weatherby lying on his back on the bed.

"Amos?"

"Clint?"

"Are you all right?"

"I can't move."

Clint walked to the bed.

"Should I get a doctor?"

"I don't need a doctor, boy," Weatherby snapped. "It was that woman you sent me."

"What about her?"

"She was marvelous. I hope you paid her enough."

"Then what she said was true?"

"If she said that somethin' great happened, somethin' that ain't happened in a long time, then, yeah, she was tellin' the truth."

"But I thought the doctor said—"

"So did I, but my body didn't care what no doctor said. With that woman naked in my bed my body sat up—*stood* up—and took notice."

"And now you can't move because of the pain?"

"Hell, there ain't no pain, boy," Weatherby said. "I can't move because she drained me!"

Clint sat on the edge of his bed and shook his head. It had never occurred to him that his friend hadn't come down for breakfast because he felt too good.

"Maybe I should arrange for her to come back to-night," he said.

"That'd be pushing my luck, don't ya think?"

"Well, maybe, but—"

"Besides," Weatherby said, cutting Clint off, "I already arranged for it."

"You old dog."

"Help me sit up, will ya?"

Weatherby put out a hand, and Clint took it and pulled the man into a seated position. It was then Clint realized that his old friend was naked—and he stunk.

He stood up and walked toward the door.

"You want her to come back you better take a bath sometime today," Clint said.

"Why don't you tell the hotel to draw me one now," Weatherby said. "A hot one. The hot water really soothes these old bones."

"You just make sure you get down there before the water gets cold."

"Okay," Weatherby said, "and Clint?"

"Yep?"

"Thanks for last night," Amos Weatherby said, and Clint thought he saw tears in his old friend's eyes. "You made a good choice."

"Take that bath," Clint said, opening the door, "and I'll see you later. I've got some things to do."

Clint didn't really have other things to do, but Amos Weatherby's tearful gratitude had made him uncomfortable; he had to get out of there.

When he reached the lobby the clerk called him over and gave him a telegram. It was Rick Hartman's reply. He knew nothing of Weatherby's condition and was sorry—"if it was true." The second half of the telegram gave him the names of three doctors in San Francisco. Clint tucked the telegram away. As far as he was concerned Weatherby was telling the truth, and there was no need for him to check with these doctors. He'd keep their names, though, for further reference. He thanked the clerk and left the hotel.

Once he was on the street, though, he decided to send a telegram back to Labyrinth, Texas, for two reasons. One, to tell Rick what he was up to, and two, to ask if Rick had any information on the whereabouts of the Dolan gang. Maybe he'd come up with something about their location that would save Clint and Weatherby the trouble of setting a trap.

He made the same arrangements to have any reply delivered to the hotel and tipped the clerk double, once for already delivering the first telegram and once for when he delivered the second.

Outside the telegraph office Clint decided it was too soon to go back to the hotel. Weatherby probably wasn't finished with his bath yet. He finally decided to kill time just by taking a walk around town. Maybe by the time he got back to the hotel Weatherby wouldn't be feeling so grateful.

TEN

When Clint finally returned to the hotel he saw Weatherby sitting in a straight-backed wooden chair out front. He was wearing clean clothes, and he smelled as if he'd come straight from a bath—which he had.

"How do you feel?" Clint asked.

"Better than I have in days," the older man said. "Pull up a chair."

Clint found another one on the other side of the board-walk and carried it over.

"What have you been doin'?" Weatherby asked.

"Sent some telegrams."

"Checkin' up on me?"

Clint shook his head.

"On the Dolan gang. Thought I might be able to find them and we wouldn't need to set out a trap."

"And?"

"No answer yet, but we have all day."

"And do what while we wait?"

"Nothing," Clint said. "That was the whole point. You get to rest a whole day."

"One day's rest is not gonna make a difference to my condition," Weatherby said.

"Well then, just do it to satisfy me, okay?"

"Sure, why not?"

"Besides," Clint added, "you'll get another chance to be with Lila tonight."

"Bein' with her will probably kill me."

"It's a great way to go."

"Not the way I want to go, though."

"I know that," Clint said. "Let me ask you something, Amos."

"Sure, go ahead."

"Why Chance Dolan?" Clint wanted to know. "I mean—no offense—but he's an old man. Why not leave him be?"

"He ain't actin' like an old man," Weatherby said. "He ain't retired. He's still plannin' robberies and sendin' his boys out to pull them off, and they're killin' people while they do it."

"Chips off the old block, huh?"

"Putting Chance behind bars—or in the ground—is gonna leave them without somebody to tell them what to do."

"What makes you think they need Chance for that?" Clint asked. "They might be happy to get rid of a bossy old man."

"I know Chance, Clint," Weatherby said. "He's got those boys trained to need him, take my word for it."

"I guess I've got to," Clint said. "You know him better than anyone."

"Fifty years," Weatherby said. "I know him, and I been chasing him for fifty years."

"And there's nothing personal in it, Amos?" Clint asked.

"It's just the law, Clint," Weatherby said. "You know it's always been the law for me."

Clint knew that Weatherby hated retiring when he did, and that was why he took up bounty hunting. In the few short years he'd done it he had become the best at it.

"I know that, Amos," Clint said. "I never knew a man who thought as much of the law as you did—and do."

"You would have been a great lawman if you'd kept at it, Clint."

"It wasn't for me, Amos. Too much politics, in both town and federal law for me."

"You just shit on 'em and keep doin' what you do, is all," Weatherby said.

"I was never able to learn that, I guess. What's this?" Clint said, straightening in his chair.

Approaching them was the clerk from the telegraph office. Rick Hartman had gotten back to him in record time, it seemed.

"Your reply, Mr. Adams," the clerk said.

"Thanks a lot."

"What's it say?" Weatherby asked. "Who's it from?"

Clint read the telegram once, then read it again. Finally, he looked at Weatherby.

"What is it?"

"Maybe you'd like to explain this to me, Amos?" Clint asked.

"Explain what?"

"Explain why Rick Hartman says that according to his information, Chance Dolan is dead and has been for five years."

Weatherby sat up in his chair so quickly that a shadow of pain crossed his face. He tried to ignore it and held out his hand.

"Mind if I see that?"

Clint handed the telegram over. Weatherby perused it, then handed it back.

"He's wrong," he said.

"Rick is hardly ever wrong about anything, Amos," Clint said.

He tucked the telegram into his pocket with the other one, the one with the doctors' names on it. Maybe he'd be using that one, after all.

"What are you trying to pull, Amos?"

"Nothin', I swear," Weatherby said. "I don't know where your friend got his information, but it's wrong."

"Amos—"

"It's wrong, Clint!"

"How can you be so sure?"

"Because I saw Chance," Weatherby said, "not three years ago!"

ELEVEN

"You want to explain that to me?" Clint demanded.

"There's nothing to explain," Weatherby said. "Chance got the better of me three years ago."

"And how did he do that?"

"Easy," Weatherby said. "I didn't know he had his sons with him."

"Tell me about it."

"It went like this. . . ."

KANSAS CITY
THREE YEARS EARLIER

Amos Weatherby was in Kansas City to celebrate his retirement from bounty hunting—only he didn't feel much like celebrating. Everyone seemed to think that, at sixty-seven he was past it, that he couldn't uphold the law anymore. He had to try to think of a way to convince them that they were wrong.

But whether he was celebrating or not he ended up in a saloon. Most men celebrated and lamented in the same fashion: getting drunk.

Weatherby was in the saloon for a couple of hours, during which he consumed three beers, when the batwing doors opened and a man walked in. Weatherby, from his back table, had to squint to make out the man's features, but he recognized him.

Chance Dolan.

He had to quell the urge to jump up from his chair. Chance Dolan had the distinction of being wanted longer than anyone in history. Weatherby could afford to wait a few more minutes before he made his move. Bringing in Chance Dolan—who Weatherby had been after for years—would show people he wasn't finished.

He had intended to let Dolan get his beer and sit down, but when the man turned away from the bar he seemed to instinctively feel Weatherby's presence. Maybe that sixth sense was part of why he'd been on the loose for so long.

Weatherby met his gaze and stood up. Everyone in the crowded saloon knew something was happening. These two grizzled veterans of the outlaw wars might have been old and gray, but they still commanded respect.

"Amos," Dolan said.

"Chance."

"I heard you was retired."

"I heard you was dead."

Dolan may have been old, but he hadn't grown foolish yet. He was holding his beer in his left hand so that his gun hand was free. Old habits died hard, as did old reprobates.

"So what do we do now?" Dolan asked.

"I got to take you in, Chance."

"I don't see no badge."

"Well, you heard right," Weatherby said. "I am retired."

"But I ain't dead," Dolan said, "and I ain't gonna be taken in."

"I was always faster than you, Chance."

"I know that, Amos, but I was always smarter."

Dolan inclined his head, and Weatherby looked behind his old foe. There were two men standing there, young men wearing their holsters slung low, identical to the way Chance Dolan stood. They even looked like Dolan.

"My sons," Dolan said.

"Good-looking boys," Weatherby said.

"Thanks. See, Amos, even when I want a beer I got to be careful."

"I can see that."

Very carefully, Chance Dolan drank down half his beer, then put the mug down on a nearby table.

"I'm gonna back out of here, Amos," he said. "If you try to stop me my boys will gun you."

"This don't end here, Chance."

Dolan shrugged.

"I been lookin' over my shoulder for you for over forty years, Amos," he said. "Why should it change now?"

Weatherby watched closely as Dolan backed out through the batwing doors, followed by his sons.

He sat down and finished his beer. . . .

THE PRESENT

"So you see," Weatherby said, "even *I* heard he was dead; but he wasn't, and he ain't. I wanted to bring him and his boys in, but along the way I brung a lot of other outlaws to justice."

Clint sat back in his chair and looked across the table at Weatherby.

"Two sons?"

"That's all I saw that day," Weatherby said.

Clint touched the pocket that held the telegram from Rick. Rarely had his friend passed on bad information, but if he was going to go along with Weatherby on this he was going to have to assume the old man knew what he was talking about.

"Okay, Amos."

"You still with me?"

"I'm still with you," Clint said.

He took the telegram out of his pocket, crumpled it up, and dropped it on the table.

TWELVE

Clint and Weatherby discussed in detail, then, how their plan would work. They were going to have to get a bank to go along with them and release word that they were bringing in a large gold shipment. The details had to be worked out. Should they announce that the shipment was coming in by train or coach? How much should they say about security?

"I think we should only mention my involvement," Weatherby said.

"You don't think Chance will be able to resist if he reads you're involved in security, do you?"

"No," Weatherby said. "He'd love to steal something this big right out from under my nose."

"Okay, so we'll mention you. You think mentioning me will keep him and his boys away?"

"I think we should play it safe and make it seem as easy as possible. With you involved it don't seem so easy."

"Okay," Clint said, "I agree again."

And so the planning continued. . . .

• • •

They walked down the street later in the day to have dinner in a café. After dinner they shared a pot of coffee. When the waiter came to collect their plates he frowned at the food left on Weatherby's. They ordered peach pie with the coffee.

"Are you feeling tired?" Clint asked.

"No," Weatherby said. "Actually I'm feeling pretty good. I think this resting stuff might have been a good idea."

"Amos, why'd you want to meet me here?" Clint asked. "We have a long way to travel, now, to get to Kansas. Why not meet there?"

"To tell you the truth," Weatherby replied slowly, "I wasn't sure I'd be able to make it to Kansas. The doctor said it would take a while to see how I reacted to the pain medication."

"Why not meet in San Francisco, then? Where you saw the doctor?"

"I wanted to test myself," Weatherby said. "Also, the doctor said the air here would be good for me."

Clint had to keep in mind that Weatherby was never above altering the truth a bit to get what he wanted. It was obvious he was ill, but all the rest of it could be some kind of ruse to get his way. So Clint believed two things: that Weatherby was sick, and that he wanted to track down Chance Dolan. Everything else Clint took with a grain of salt.

After dinner they walked back to the hotel, and Weatherby announced he was going to go to his room.

"I been sittin' on hard chairs all day," he said. "The doctor said sooner or later I'm gonna have to sit on pillows or something soft."

"That'll leave out horseback."

"Oh, yeah," Weatherby said, "this will probably be my last hurrah on a horse. Too bad, too. I always loved ridin' the trail."

"I know you did."

"That was the only thing I liked better about bounty hunting than wearing a badge."

They stopped in front of the hotel and Weatherby said, "You want to leave at first light?"

"If you're up to it."

"I'll be up to it."

"I'll pick up a few supplies, enough to get us to the nearest railroad."

"Fine."

Weatherby started to go in and Clint said, "Take it easy on that young woman, old man."

"Yeah, yeah," Weatherby said; waving. "She better go easy on me, I think."

Clint shook his head as Weatherby disappeared through the door, then turned and walked to the mercantile store to pick up their supplies.

As with the day before, Kate's father chose to disappear when Clint entered.

"Did you give him the happy news yet?" Clint asked her.

"What news?"

"That I'm leaving in the morning."

"Is it definite?"

"Yes."

She pouted. "Then I don't consider that good news."

"*He* will, though."

"Will we have time to say good-bye tonight?" she asked.

"I'll make time," he promised. "For now, though, I need to pick up some supplies. . . ."

THIRTEEN

Arch Dolan watched Belinda walk across the saloon floor with a tray of drinks in her hands. She knew he was watching and moved her hips accordingly. She had good hips and big, firm breasts that threatened to fall from her blouse when she bent over to serve the drinks.

"You need anything else, Arch, honey?" she asked, straightening up and smiling. She had full lips that she painted red for him, because she knew it drove him crazy. He'd never known a woman before whose upper and lower lips were the same fullness.

"Not right now, Belinda," he said. "Maybe later."

She ignored the three other men at the table and spoke only to him.

"You waitin' on your brother Sammy?"

"Yep, I sure am."

"He's upstairs with Monica."

"Which one is Monica?"

She liked when he pretended he didn't know who any of the other girls were.

51

"The blonde with skinny legs and blue eyes."

"My little brother," Arch said, "he likes them skinny women."

"I know," Belinda said.

"Me, I like more meat on a woman."

She smiled, licked her red lips, and said, "I know. You let me know if you need anything else, you hear?"

"Oh, I hear, Belinda," he said. "I hear real good."

As she walked away Ken Harvey leaned forward and asked, "Why'd you pretend you don't know who Monica is? Hell, you been with her as much as me. That gal's skinny, but she's got a mouth—"

"Shut up, Ken!" Arch hissed. "Belinda hasn't been here as long as Monica, so she don't know about that, and I don't want her to."

"What if Monica tells her?"

"Monica knows I'd bust her neck if she opened her mouth . . . for the wrong reason, that is."

That made the other men at the table laugh.

"Your brother's been up there a long time, Arch," Hal Sterling said.

"Yeah, well, he's young," Arch said. "He can last longer than we can."

"Not longer than me," Dick Easy said.

"You tell him that, Dick."

"Not me," Easy said. "Your little brother's crazy, Arch."

"Don't let Pa hear you talkin' like that," Arch said. "He'll kill you."

"Don't worry, I won't," Easy said. "That old man scares me more than your brothers."

"So I'm the only one you ain't scared of, Dick?" Arch asked.

"Hell, I ain't a-scared of you, Arch," Easy said, then added quickly, "I respect you."

Arch wasn't sure if that was the same thing or not, but he let it go.

Arch Dolan knew he was the smartest one in his family. Sammy would be smart if Sterling hadn't been right about him. That crazy streak in him made him do dumb things. Their older brother, Leon—well, he was trail smart, but he was also the old man's right hand, so he didn't do much thinkin' for himslf. And the old man, well, he was just behind the times. Arch, he knew he was the only one who could lead this gang in a new direction—if he could get them to follow him. The problem was they were all afraid of the other three Dolans. Maybe, though, he could turn their *respect* for him to his advantage.

Like the newspaper he had in front of him, the *Atchison Times*. It had a story in it about a gold shipment that was being sent from Kansas City, Missouri, to Topeka, Kansas. It didn't say exactly how much there was, but Kansas City and Topeka were good-size towns with decent banks. This had to be a big shipment.

"You still readin' that story about the gold?" Harvey asked.

"Yep."

"You think your old man is gonna go for it?" Easy asked.

"I don't know," Arch said. "He usually doesn't go for anything that's my idea."

"Then how you gonna get him to go for this?" Easy persisted.

"I'll just have to make him think it's his idea," Arch said.

"And how are you gonna do that?" Sterling asked.

"Just leave that to me," Arch said. "I'll think of somethin'."

"And if he don't go for it?" Harvey wanted to know.

"Let's just say I ain't about to let somethin' like this get by," Arch replied. "I'd just need some men who feel the same way."

"Well," Ken Harvey said, picking up one of the fresh beers Belinda had just brought—the one her left breast had almost fallen into—"you can count me in, Arch."

Arch Dolan looked at Sterling and Easy, but they looked away, making it clear that they weren't yet ready to follow him.

Soon, though, he thought. *Soon.*

FOURTEEN

Clint and Amos Weatherby were in Topeka, reading the same article in the *Atchison Times*. They were in a saloon, and Weatherby was not looking good.

When they first left Prescott he had looked fine. Another night with Lila had made him feel like a new man again. This lasted all the way to Kansas City, where they disembarked from the train and got hotel rooms in the Kansas House. They stayed only long enough to find a bank manager who would go along with their plan: a man Weatherby had known for years, who owed him a favor. They were about the same age, so the man said he would go along with them so he could repay the favor while they were both still alive.

After that they had to ride from Kansas City to Topeka. It wasn't that long a ride, but it seemed to have taken its toll on Weatherby, who had not been looking well for the past few days.

"Think this will do it?" Clint asked Weatherby.

"I hope so," the other man replied. "Don't know how much longer I can last."

Clint was worried. If this didn't work, then they were

either going to have to go into Missouri to look for Chance Dolan and his boys or come up with a different plan. Right now, Amos Weatherby looked as if he'd never survive the ride.

"You got medicine left?"

Weatherby nodded and said, "My last bottle."

"Is that going to be enough, Amos?"

"It'll have to be."

"Why don't you go back to the hotel and get some rest? Maybe even take some medicine."

Weatherby sighed. "I guess so. Seems to be all I do these past few days, lie in bed and wait for the pain to stop. You know . . . sometimes my rifle looks like my best friend."

He got up and walked out, and Clint knew exactly what he meant. Rather than waste away from the inside out even he might choose the barrel of a gun as an alternative. Maybe that was what Doc Holliday had been doing all these years, just trying to get himself killed to put him out of his misery.

Clint looked at the newspaper again, then put it down and went to the bar for another beer.

Arch Dolan looked up and saw his older brother, Leon, come through the batwing doors of the saloon. He knew the old man had sent Leon to get them.

The old man didn't scare Arch anymore, and he could handle little brother Sammy. Leon, though, was a different story. He was firmly in the old man's pocket, and if the old man told him to kill his brothers, Leon would. That made him scary.

Leon spotted them and came over to their table.

"Time to go, gents," he said.

"Come on, Leon," Arch said, "have one beer with us."

"Pa wants us all back in Warsaw tonight."

"We'll go," Arch said. "Just have one beer."

Leon looked around the saloon, but Arch knew he wasn't even considering his suggestion.

"Where's Sammy?"

"He's upstairs, Leon," Dick Easy said.

Leon looked at Easy, then Sterling, then Ken Harvey.

"You boys better get started back."

Easy and Sterling stood up right away. Ken Harvey waited for a slight nod from Arch before he, too, got up and left.

Leon looked at Arch.

"You want to go up and get him, or should I?"

Arch hesitated. He wondered if he should show the newspaper to Leon or not. He decided not. Even though he was twenty-five and Leon was only two years older, he didn't feel particularly close to his brother. Now, Sammy, he was nineteen, but seemed a lot younger. No, Arch was alone in the Dolan family, and he didn't like it. It was time he did something about it.

He folded up the newspaper instead of showing it to Leon and said, "I'll get him."

Arch went upstairs and opened the door to Monica's room. The first thing he saw was her naked, skinny rump sticking up in the air. Sammy was lying in bed on his back with his legs spread, and she was between them, his dick in her mouth.

"Time to go, Sammy."

"Wha—" Sammy said, in a daze.

Monica let his dick slide wetly from her mouth and looked over her shoulder at Arch.

"Hi, Arch, honey."

"Hello, Monica. Come on, Sammy, Leon's downstairs. Let's go."

"Awright, awright," Sammy said. "Jeez, guy can't even get laid around here."

"He already came twice," Monica said to Arch.

"That's more than I wanted to know, Monica," Arch said, as Sammy slid off the bed, showing his brother more than he wanted to see.

Monica remained in position, with her little pink butthole winking at Arch, and said, "What about you, Arch? Want some?" She slid her hand over her rump and touched that pink hole with two of her fingers.

"Not tonight, Monica, thanks," Arch said, but his dick was getting hard already. He knew from past experience how tight that hole was, how it gripped a man's cock, but he was concentrating on Belinda these days, not skinny Monica.

Monica sighed and rolled over on the bed to face Arch, who could now see her skinny breasts with their enormous nipples.

"Still after Belinda, Arch?"

"None of your business, Monica."

"You know," she said, "you won't get as much from her for free as you will from me for five dollars."

"I'll take my chances."

"She ain't as good as me."

"Sammy, I'll wait for you downstairs."

"I'm ready," Sammy said, hopping on one foot, pulling on his second boot.

Monica reached out and grabbed Sammy's shirttail, yanking on it. Sammy was so skinny she almost knocked him over. They made a good pair, Arch thought. They'd have real skinny kids.

"You can't go until you pay me, Sammy, honey."

"Leggo my shirt, Mon!" he snapped.

"Pay up," she repeated firmly.

"Awright, here." Sammy threw some crumpled bills on the bed.

"There's only four here, Sammy. The price was five."

"That's all I got," he said. "Arch? You got a dollar?"

"Go on downstairs, Sammy," Arch said, "Leon is waiting."

"I'm goin'."

As his younger brother went down the hall, Arch pulled a dollar from his pocket, walked over to Monica, and handed it to her. She took it in her right hand and cupped his crotch with her left.

"Well," she said, "it's nice to know you're still interested."

"Good night, Monica," he said, and went down to join his brothers.

FIFTEEN

In all his travels Clint had never stopped in Topeka, Kansas, before. He took the time to walk around and get acquainted a bit before going back to the saloon he'd been in earlier with Weatherby. He went to the bar and ordered a beer.

"Gonna be stayin' long?" the bartender asked.

"A few days, maybe."

"Saw you sittin' with Weatherby before."

"You recognized him, did you?"

"Oh, sure," the bartender said. "Can't get to my age— I'm fifty-five—without knowin' who Amos Weatherby is. 'Sides, he's gonna be running security for that gold shipment that's comin' in."

"You read about that in the newspaper?" Clint asked. He had the paper in his back pocket.

"It's in the paper?"

"Well, yeah," Clint said, taking the paper out and spreading it on the bar.

"Oh, the Atchison paper."

"It's in a few others, as well."

"Well, that ain't where I heard about it," the bartender

said. "Most of the people in this town have known about it for some time. I'm kinda surprised they hired Weatherby, though. I mean, he is a little—well, long in the tooth."

"I guess they have confidence in him," Clint said. "Tell me again how you know about this."

"Heard about it a few weeks ago," the man said. "Can't have somethin' that big happening in town without it gettin' around, can ya?"

"No, I guess not."

Clint turned to leave the saloon.

"Hey, ain'tcha gonna finish your beer?"

"Not right now," he said. "I've got a skinny neck to wring."

Clint entered Weatherby's room without knocking. They'd decided he should have a key, just in case something happened.

"Come on, you sick old man, wake up!"

"Huh? What?"

Weatherby woke abruptly, and his pallor seemed bad, yellow as opposed to the pale he'd been earlier. Clint immediately felt badly for waking him up, but he didn't like being lied to.

"Tell me again about this gold shipment," Clint said.

"What the hell are you—"

"This made-up gold shipment that we're hoping the Dolan gang will go for. Tell me more about it."

Weatherby frowned, sat up painfully—Clint didn't offer to help—and wiped some sludge out of his eyes.

"This is one of the lousy things about gettin' old," he said, "havin' to wipe this stuff out of your eyes even after a nap."

"Never mind that, Amos," Clint said. "Talk to me.

How come the people of this town knew about the gold shipment before it hit the papers?''

"I was gonna tell you . . .''

"Tell me what? That this gold shipment is real?''

"I didn't think you'd hear—''

"Why would you lie to me about a thing like that?'' Clint exploded. "And what else have you lied to me about?''

"Nothin'! Stop shoutin', will ya? I got a headache.''

He reached for the bottle of medicine on the table next to the bed. Clint watched while he tried to pour himself a spoonful, then gave up and just swigged it from the bottle.

"Gimme a minute, Clint,'' he said, lying back down. "I'll tell ya all about it.''

Clint gave him a minute, but by then the older man was asleep again.

"Shit,'' Clint said beneath his breath. He didn't want to wake him again, so he was just going to have to push his anger away and wait for Weatherby to wake up and tell him what the hell was going on.

SIXTEEN

Clint was sitting in the lobby of the hotel reading a newspaper when Weatherby came down. This paper had nothing in it about the gold shipment, but it was several days old. When he saw Weatherby he left the paper on the sofa and got up to meet him.

"I owe you an explanation," Weatherby said. His pallor was better, and he didn't look as if he was in as much pain as before.

"You look better."

"I feel better," he said, "but let's go get some coffee and I'll explain."

They went into the hotel dining room, sat down, and ordered.

"I didn't want you to know I was getting paid for this job."

"What job?"

"Security for the gold shipment."

"How long have you had it?"

"About a month. They've been planning this shipment longer than that. I heard they were looking for someone to arrange security."

"And you couldn't resist taking a job like that this close to Missouri, figuring it would draw out Chance and his boys."

"Right."

"Well, all of that makes sense, Amos, except for lying to me about it."

"I thought you might think I was just doin' it for the money."

"Come on," Clint said. "Why would I think that of you? You never cared about money before."

"This is different."

"What is?"

"There's something else I didn't tell you."

Clint hesitated a moment, then said, "Amos, I hope this is the last thing."

"It is." Weatherby licked his lips before continuing. "There may be an operation that could help me live a little longer."

"How much longer?"

"I don't know," Weatherby said, "but here I am seventy years old, and I find I'm not ready to go, Clint. It might happen to you when you reach my age."

"*If* I reach your age," Clint said.

"Whatever . . . I want whatever I can get. A few years, a few months, maybe, without pain . . ."

"Amos . . . is it worth having them cut you open?"

"Yes," Weatherby said, "I think it is, but I need the money I'm being paid for this job."

"So why did you need me?"

"I don't get paid unless the gold gets through. I needed somebody I could count on to watch my back, but somebody I could trust not to be tempted by the gold. You're the only one I could think of."

"I suppose I should be flattered by that."

"Clint . . . look, no more lies from here on out, okay? Don't walk away from me now."

"Nobody said anything about walking away, Amos," Clint said.

"Then you'll stick with me?"

"Yes," Clint said, "but there's one thing I don't understand. Why take the risk of facing Chance and his gang?"

"Because if I don't make it," Weatherby explained, "I don't want *him* to make it. It irks me to think I'll be dead and he'll still be robbing banks and killing people. Clint, I want to deliver that gold and take him down before I go."

"Well," Clint said, "we'll see what we can do to make that happen."

SEVENTEEN

"There's just one problem," Weatherby said.

"What?" Clint asked expectantly.

"This is not a lie," Weatherby was quick to point out, "just a slight problem."

"What's that?"

"One of us has to go back to Kansas City and ride along with the gold."

"One of us? Meaning you?"

"I wish," Weatherby said. "No, I don't think I can make it, Clint."

"All right, Amos. I'll go. Uh, have you been paid for this job yet? I mean, did you get any money up-front?"

"Just some expense money."

"And did you use that money to hire other men?"

"Uh, no."

"I'll be guarding this gold alone?"

"No, no," Weatherby said, "there'll be some bank guards along, too."

"How many?"

"Well, two from Kansas City, and then halfway here they'll hand it over to two guards from Topeka."

"I'll want to meet the Topeka guards so I know them on sight."

"Of course."

"And when I get to Kansas City I want to meet those guards."

"I'll arrange it."

"Are there any other surprises?"

"Only one," Weatherby said.

"What?"

"If I wake up tomorrow and decide to go with you."

"That *would* be a surprise," Clint admitted.

Weatherby shifted uncomfortably in his chair and muttered, "It'd be a goddamned miracle!"

They walked from the hotel over to the Topeka Savings & Loan to meet the bank manager, Edward Whiting.

"Well, Mr. Adams," he said, extending his hand after Weatherby had made the introductions, "I must say we're certainly happy to have you aboard. I know your reputation well."

"I'm just here to help."

"Frankly," Whiting said, "the board was on the fence about giving Mr. Weatherby this job until he told us you would be part of the package."

"Oh?" Clint asked, giving Weatherby a sidelong glance. "He assured you of that, did he?"

"Yes, indeed," Whiting said. "We were very happy to know the Gunsmith would be guarding our gold."

Whiting was white-haired and pale, a man in his sixties with teeth yellowed from many years of smoking, so when he smiled as widely as he was at the moment it was not a pretty sight.

"Mr. Whiting, I'd like to meet the two guards who will be riding with me."

"Of course, of course," Whiting said. "I can have them here in an hour."

"Good, I'll come back."

"They'll, uh, be picking you and the gold up halfway. Is that still the plan?"

"Oh, yes," Clint said, "that's still the plan."

"Excellent," Whiting said. "Then I will see you here in one hour."

They shook hands again and left the bank.

"You told them I was in on this weeks before you spoke to me?" Clint demanded when they were outside.

"I had to," Weatherby said. "They didn't want to give the job to a man of my age."

"Did you know then that you were sick?"

"No," Weatherby said. "I was feeling poorly, but I didn't see a doctor until I went to San Francisco."

"Amos, what made you think I wouldn't turn down this job?"

"I know you, boy," Weatherby said. "I knew you wouldn't let me down."

"Have you always been this devious and I just didn't see it?"

"It was the hero worship," Weatherby said. "It got in the way of the truth."

"Hero worship," Clint muttered.

"Come on, lad. I'll buy you a beer and we can kill the hour."

"You're having a beer?"

"Well," Weatherby said, "maybe a warm one."

"Come back to finish that beer?" the bartender asked Clint.

"I think I'll have a fresh one," Clint said.

"I'll have one, too," Weatherby added.

"Sure thing, Mr. Weatherby."

The barman drew two beers and brought them back.

"Did you wring that skinny neck you was talkin' about?" he asked Clint.

Clint picked up his beer and said, "Not yet, but the day isn't done."

They walked to a table and sat down. The saloon was only half full, but Clint sat with his back to the wall, and Weatherby slanted his chair so he could see the whole place.

"Tell me something," Clint said.

"What?"

"Why are we bringing the gold in by wagon and not by train?"

"They'd expect that," Weatherby said. "We don't want to make this too easy for them, or they might get suspicious."

"Seems to me Chance would be wondering the same thing," Clint said.

"You think so?"

Clint nodded.

"Well, maybe . . ." Weatherby said. "But we can't change the plan in midstream."

"When does the gold have to come through?"

"Well, if you go to Kansas City tomorrow, meet the guards—you already met the bank manager when we were there two days ago—you should be able to start back with the gold day after tomorrow."

"How did the gold get to Kansas City?"

"By trail with a bunch of armed guards supplied by the railroad."

"We could have brought it here the same way."

"Too hard," Weatherby said. "Chance would pass it up."

"What if Chance doesn't know about this shipment?"

"It's been in most of the Missouri papers."

"What if he doesn't read the papers?"

"One of his boys will see it and show it to him. Don't worry, he'll know about it."

"If he doesn't," Clint said, "all these plans—and lies—will be wasted."

"Be a shame to waste good lies," Weatherby commented.

EIGHTEEN

"Hey, Pa, look at this!"

The Dolan gang was in their house in Warsaw, Missouri: Chance, the three boys, and the other three members of their gang. Arch looked up at the sound of Sammy's voice and saw his younger brother carrying a newspaper over to their father.

Chance Dolan was a big, tall man, but where he was once barrel-chested, now he was painfully thin. He was seventy, which meant he had his three sons late in life. Arch and Leon had the same mother; Sammy's mother had been a girl of twenty-three, Chance fifty-one when Sammy was born, and the birthing had killed her. Sammy was always too dumb to realize that his father held that against him—to the point where he discounted anything his young son ever said.

"What is it?" Chance asked wearily.

"A gold shipment is being sent from Kansas City to Topeka," Sammy said. "Sounds like an easy one for us."

Arch held his breath. He knew that since hitting the shipment was Sammy's idea there was a good chance that Chance would veto it, but he held his breath anyway.

"Here, take a look," Sammy said, thrusting the newspaper at his father.

"Forget it."

"What?"

"I said forget it."

"Why?"

"Because gold shipments are well guarded, that's why," Chance said. "Because you'd probably get your fool head blown off trying to steal it."

"No, I wouldn't," Sammy said. "Hey, why don't you let me take the boys and grab it, and you stay here?"

"How's it bein' shipped?"

"I don't know."

"Does it say?"

Sammy scanned the article again and then said, "No."

"So how are you gonna find out?"

"By goin' to Kansas City!" Sammy said proudly, after taking two full seconds to think about it.

"And are we wanted half as much anyplace else as we are in Kansas City?"

"Uh, no."

"So you'd be recognized right away, wouldn't you?"

"I guess."

"You guess."

Chance was seated at a table while Sammy hovered over him, and even though he'd lost most of the bulk he carried all his life, he was still a strong man. He backhanded his youngest son from his seated position and knocked him right off his feet. The newspaper flew from his hand.

"Forget it!"

Sammy wiped his mouth with the back of his hand, saw a smear of blood, and started blubbering. He just sat there on the floor with tears running down his face, which disgusted Chance.

"Get him out of here, Leon."

"Yes, Pa."

Leon pulled Sammy to his feet and dragged him out the door.

"Anybody else want to go off on their own and grab a gold shipment?" Chance asked.

"Not me," Sterling said.

"Me, either, Chance," Dick Easy said.

"You're the boss, Pa," Arch said, because he knew that was that his father wanted to hear. "I'm goin' out for some air."

"I need a smoke," Ken Harvey said, and got up to follow Arch.

Outside they saw Leon tending to Sammy, washing his face from a horse trough.

"Those two get along too good," Harvey said.

"Let's go this way," Arch said, and they walked in the other direction.

When they each had a cigarette going, Harvey said, "That was close."

"I know," Arch said. "Too close. I didn't think Pa would even talk to Sammy about it. Good thing it was Sammy, though, who saw the article, and not Leon. Pa woulda listened to Leon."

"So now the gold is still ours to take."

"Yeah, but not just the two of us."

"I can get a couple of men," Harvey said.

"Yeah? Who?"

"A couple of fellas who used to ride with my pa and my uncle."

Arch thought a few minutes and then said, "All right, but we need them fast. We'll have to make some excuse to go to Kansas City tomorrow. We got to find out how that gold is being shipped.''

''Your pa was right about bein' wanted in Kansas City,'' Harvey said. ''Any of the four of you goes there you'll be recognized.''

''That's right,'' Arch said, slapping Ken Harvey on the back, ''but you won't.''

NINETEEN

When Clint rode into Kansas City again he thought about how he'd been there three or four times in a year's time. After this, he thought, he was going to stay away from Kansas City for a while.

He registered at the Kansas House and went directly to the bank. The manager was waiting for him; Weatherby had sent a telegram ahead.

"The two guards who will be riding with you will be here shortly, Mr. Adams," Henry Robbins said. "Can I get you a drink?"

"No, I'm fine," Clint said.

Henry Robbins was the man who had owed Weatherby a favor for a very long time.

"This will be my last year as bank manager, you know," he said. "They're making me retire."

"I'm sure you've earned you retirement, Mr. Robbins," Clint said.

"Oh, yes, I have, it's just that—well, I've managed to outlive not only my wife but my two sons, as well. And they died young, so there are no daughters-in-law and no grandchildren."

"That's a shame."

"And I really feel very fit, you see," Robbins went on. "I could easily work another five years. By then I'd be seventy and probably ready to retire."

"But you're not ready now."

"No, I'm afraid not."

Clint decided to change the subject.

"Is the gold here now, Mr. Robbins?"

"Oh, yes, it's in the vault. Do you wish to see it?"

"Please," Clint said. "Just a glance."

"Follow me, then."

Robbins opened the vault under the watchful eye of an armed bank guard. Clint stepped into the vault with him and eyed the gold bars. He felt no particular thrill while looking at them. He preferred folding money.

"The gold will be in six chests and loaded onto a buckboard."

"I'll want to be here during loading," Clint said.

"Very well."

"And I'll want the other two men there, too."

"No problem."

"I'd like to load before the bank opens, at eight."

"I'll arrange it," Robbins said. "Shall we go back to my office now?"

"Yes."

They had just sat down again when there was a knock on the door and a pretty young teller stuck her head in.

"The guards are here, sir."

"Send them in, Miss White, and thank you."

"Yes, sir."

She withdrew and a moment later two burly men came through the door. Both Clint and Henry Robbins got to their feet.

"Gentlemen, this is Clint Adams. Mr. Adams, George Starke and Frank Packer."

"A pleasure to meet you, Mr. Adams," Packer said as they shook hands.

"Just call me Clint," he replied, shaking hands with Starke.

The men weren't in uniform, but they were dressed similarly. Dark clothes and hats, a gun and holster. The meeting was almost identical to the one that had taken place in the bank in Topeka.

"Do you men know the whole story?" Clint asked.

"Sir?" Starke said.

Clint looked at Robbins.

"I thought you should brief them yourself."

"I see," Clint said. "Well, maybe we should go and get a drink and take care of that."

Neither man complained about having a drink, so they left the bank and went to the nearest saloon.

When they reached the outskirts of Kansas City, Arch Dolan and Ken Harvey reined in their horses.

"All right," Arch said, "you ride on in and see what you can find out. I'm gonna make a cold camp here and wait for you."

"Right."

"Remember, all we need to know is when they're gonna load the gold, and then we'll know when they're leaving. Then we just have to follow them and wait for the right moment."

"I got it."

"And you'll find the men you were talkin' about?" Arch asked.

"They're usually in Kansas City, if they're not off on a job."

"What if they are?"

"I was here a week ago and they didn't have any prospects," Harvey replied.

"Well, let's hope they didn't come up with any. Okay, go."

As Ken Harvey rode off toward Kansas City, Arch Dolan dismounted and walked his horse to a clearing where he'd make camp. Pretty soon everybody would know that it wasn't only Chance Dolan who could plan big jobs and pull them off.

"So we're expecting to be hit?" Starke asked.

"That's right."

"And there are only three of us?" Packer asked. "And how many of them?"

"As I understand it, Chance Dolan might have two or three sons," Clint said. "As for our number, I've managed to increase that."

"How?" Packer asked.

"Well, I've asked the Topeka bank security men to ride along with us instead of meeting us halfway, and I'd also like you to ride all the way to Topeka."

Packer and Starke exchanged a glance. They were both in their thirties, strapping big men. They were not gunmen by any means, but they knew how to use their weapons.

"You'll be paid extra, of course," Clint said.

That changed the looks on their faces, and they nodded enthusiastically.

"The other two men, however, will not ride alongside us; they'll be hidden."

"So we're setting a trap," Packer said.

"Right. Now, just in case they somehow know our plans, when we get halfway the other two guards will ride with me, and you two will ride along, unseen. You can ride, can't you?"

"That's not a problem," Starke said.

"Very well," Packer added.

"Good. As I understand it, the gold is already in the bank, so we'll meet there tomorrow morning before the bank opens, at eight."

"We'll be there, sir," Packer said.

"And you're going to have to stop that," Clint said. "Just call me Clint."

"No problem," Starke said.

"Yes, si—uh, I mean, okay," Parker said.

"Then drink up and spend the rest of the day doing whatever you want to do, but show up tomorrow at the bank at eight, and don't be hungover."

"These are the last drinks we'll have today," Packer said.

"Have you fellas worked together before?"

"We're partners," Starke replied. "We always work together."

"Good," Clint said. "I'll see you boys tomorrow, then."

Clint left the saloon and the two security men remained behind. He didn't know how serious they were about not having any more drinks, but he wasn't going to watch them to make sure. If they knew their jobs, he could count on them to be there tomorrow and to be ready.

Ken Harvey watched the man exit the saloon, leaving behind the two bank guards. He waited a few minutes, then walked over to the table where they were sitting, carrying fresh beers.

"You boys look thirsty," he said.

Packer and Starke looked up at him, and Packer said,

''Hey, Ken, we ain't seen you in . . . what? A week? Have a seat.''

Harvey sat down with the two men who, as younger men, had ridden with his uncle and his father before Amos Weatherby had put them away.

TWENTY

"You're kidding."

Arch Dolan looked across the fire at Ken Harvey and couldn't believe his luck.

"I don't believe it," he said.

"Believe it," Harvey said. "They couldn't come up with any good jobs to pull so they got jobs as security men for the bank."

"How'd they manage that?"

"They rode with my uncle and father for a few years, but they never got arrested. When the gang was caught they weren't there."

"So they don't have a record."

"Right."

"This is too good to be true." Even his father had never run into this kind of luck. It was an omen. It had to be.

"But wait," Harvey said, drawing out the suspense, "there's more."

"What's that?" Arch replied impatiently.

"The man who hired 'em is Clint Adams."

"*What?*"

Harvey nodded.

"The Gunsmith is guarding this gold?" Arch asked.

"Now here's the good part," Harvey said. "The Gunsmith is working with—get this—Amos Weatherby."

"Weatherby?" Arch asked. "I thought he was dead."

"Well, he ain't," Harvey said. "He's in.Topeka waiting for this gold to get there."

"Weatherby," Arch repeated. "Him and my old man go way back."

"I know."

"And ain't he the one stuck your old man in Leavenworth?"

"Yep," Harvey said, "he got the whole gang, except Starke and Packer."

"Well, this ties up real good then, don't it?" Arch asked. "When I tell my old man we scored the gold, *and* I killed Amos Weatherby, there ain't no way he can be anything but impressed."

"Don't forget Adams."

"Oh, shit," Arch said. "I did forget. We'll have to take care of him, too."

"It shouldn't be too hard," Harvey said. "He don't know Packer and Starke are with us, and we know their plan. There's gonna be two more riding along, but out of sight."

"So we have to take care of them first."

"Right."

"And Packer and Starke can take care of Adams."

"Uh . . . no."

"Whaddya mean, no?"

"They won't go up against him alone."

"Why not? All they got to do is backshoot the son of a bitch."

"They're afraid to try," Harvey said.

"I thought you said we could rely on them."

"We can, but they didn't bargain for going up against the Gunsmith alone—and neither did I, for that matter."

"So what do you suggest?"

"We'll have to take care of him together," Harvey said. "The four of us."

"You think the four of us can take the Gunsmith?"

"Well, sure, why not? You're pretty good with a gun, Arch. You can be the one who backshoots him."

"Okay," Arch said, "then I get to kill Adams *and* Weatherby."

"You'll have a helluva rep when this job is finished, Arch," Harvey said. "A helluva rep."

"Bigger than my father," Arch said.

"That's for sure."

"When are they loadin' the gold?"

"Eight A.M."

"Okay, then we better get some sleep," Arch decided. "We're gonna want to be where we can see them by seven-thirty."

"This was a great idea, Arch," Harvey commented, rolling himself up in his blanket. "A great idea."

"Yeah," Arch said, "it is a great idea."

"When this is over, I can tell my old man and my uncle that we took care of Weatherby."

"How much credit you want, Ken?" Arch asked. "You can have a rep, too, you know."

"Don't want one," Harvey said. "I just want to get Weatherby for what he did to my family."

"We'll get him, all right," Arch said. "We'll get him good."

Harvey rolled over and closed his eyes, thinking about the looks on his father's and uncle's faces when he told them that he fixed Amos Weatherby once and for all.

Arch Dolan rolled over and thought about the look on his father's face, and the faces of his brothers, when they all found out about the job he'd engineered, about killing Weatherby *and* the Gunsmith.

No way, he thought, *they could be anything* but *impressed.*

TWENTY-ONE

Clint got to the bank before the two security guards did. The manager, however, was there already and opened the door for him. Inside was the bank guard he had seen the day before, when he'd gone into the vault.

"Good morning," Henry Robbins said.

"Morning," Clint said, and nodded to the bank guard, who stood with his hand on his gun.

"The two guards should be along any minute," Robbins said. "They're picking up the buckboard from the livery stable."

"Good, I was wondering about that."

"Did you sleep well?" Robbins continued, making conversation.

"I slept real well, thanks."

"I have some coffee in my office. Care for some?"

"Thanks, I would."

Clint followed Robbins into his office, where the man poured him a cup.

"You have something on your mind, Mr. Robbins?" he asked.

"It shows?"

"It showed yesterday," Clint said.

"Mr. Adams," Robbins said, "I, uh, this gold shipment . . . uh, I believe I can use the successful transfer of this gold to possibly prolong my career with the bank."

"I hope you can," Clint said.

"Yes, well, it's possible I might need your help to do it."

"What can I do?"

"Well, you can tell them at the other end how, uh, *instrumental* I was in the transfer of the gold."

"Okay."

In that moment, Clint realized that neither bank manager—this one or the one in Topeka—knew that Weatherby was using this gold shipment to draw out the Dolan gang. All Robbins had done—as a favor—was help Weatherby get the job transporting the gold.

"I'll do that, Mr. Robbins."

"I'd appreciate that, sir," Robbins said. "See, I'm still young enough to do my job."

"I believe you are," Clint said, and then added, "and you make a mean cup of coffee."

It was a lie, but if it made the man feel good where was the harm? As long as he didn't have to drink any more of it—ever!

The bank guard stuck his head in the door and said, "They're here, sir."

"Excellent," Robbins said. "Let's get this gold on the buckboard."

Clint stopped the man's exit by saying, "Mr. Robbins."

"Yes?"

"Can you tell me why we don't have an armored wagon for this transfer?"

"You should talk to Amos about that, Mr. Adams,"

Robbins answered. "He said he couldn't get one."

Clint frowned, wondering if Weatherby had even tried. Maybe he thought using an armored car would put Chance Dolan off.

"I'll do that as soon as I get back to Topeka."

Clint watched as the two security guards loaded the gold onto the buckboard one chest at a time, under the watchful eye of the bank guard.

"I haven't asked," he said to Robbins, "but whose gold is this, anyway?"

Robbins looked at Clint blankly for a moment, then said, "I can't say that I know for sure, Mr. Adams. My instructions were simply to see to the transfer. I assumed the gold belonged to the bank."

"Which one?"

"Both banks have the same owner."

"I see. So they're really just transferring it from one bank to another."

"That's as I understand it."

Clint wasn't sure that anyone was understanding anything correctly. Maybe Amos Weatherby was the only one who really knew what was going on.

"Jesus," Ken Harvey said, as he and Arch Dolan watched the gold being loaded onto the wagon, "six chests of it? Do you know how much that is?"

"Ain't got the faintest idea," Arch said, "but I want it."

"This might be the biggest gold shipment in history," Harvey said.

Neither man wondered why such a shipment wasn't being sent by train or in an armored wagon. Chance Dolan would have asked those two questions right away.

''We're gonna have to take the whole wagon,'' Harvey said.

''I figured that, Ken,'' Arch said, feeling superior to the other man.

''We won't be able to move real fast.''

''If this goes right,'' Arch said, ''ain't nobody gonna be followin' us.''

''Yeah, that's right.''

They watched as the last chest was set on the buckboard.

''I hope that thing can hold all that weight,'' Harvey commented.

''It must be reinforced,'' Arch said, again demonstrating his superior intellect.

''Yeah, you're probably right.''

''Come on,'' Arch said, getting to his feet. They were able to see the bank clearly from the top of a rise just outside of town.

''Where to?''

''We're gonna get a little ahead of them and see if we can spot them other two guards.''

''We won't lose 'em, will we?'' Ken Harvey asked, worriedly.

''Not a chance, Ken,'' Arch said, ''not a chance.''

''I just need you to sign this receipt that the gold was loaded,'' Mr. Robbins said to Clint.

He handed it to Clint, who signed it.

One of the guards was going to drive the buckboard while the other was on horseback. Clint walked to Duke and mounted the big, black gelding.

''Have a safe trip,'' Mr. Robbins said.

''We'll try, Mr. Robbins,'' Clint said. ''Thanks for your help.''

"Don't forget what we talked about, eh?" Robbins said.

"Don't worry," Clint assured him, "I won't." He looked at the two security guards and said, "Let's move out."

TWENTY-TWO

"Somebody's behind us," Arch Dolan said.

"The guards?"

They still hadn't spotted the two extra guards and were trying to move as carefully and quietly as they could.

"No," Arch said, "somebody else."

"Who?"

"Let's find out."

Arch Dolan and Ken Harvey moved into some brush and waited to see who was tailing them. Soon they were able to hear plainly a horse approaching, closer and closer, until a rider went right by their hiding place.

"Hold it!" Arch snapped, riding out from hiding with his gun drawn. Harvey was right behind him, also holding his gun.

"What the—" Harvey said.

"Sammy!" Arch exclaimed. "What the hell are you doin' here?"

Sammy Dolan smiled.

"You all think I'm pretty dumb, but I knew somethin' was goin' on with you two."

"You been tailin' us the whole time?" Arch asked.

"Except when Ken went into Kansas City," Sammy said. "Then I stayed with you, just outside your camp."

"You know what we're doin'?"

"Sure I know," Sammy said. "You're goin' after that gold shipment. It was my idea, you know. I want to be cut in."

"You're an idiot, Sammy. I had this idea way before you saw the article in the paper."

"Prove it."

"I don't have to prove it," Arch snapped. "You're goin' back home."

"I'm goin' with you," Sammy said. "If I go back home I'm gonna tell Pa the whole story."

"Go ahead," Arch said, "tell him. You don't even know the whole story."

"I know enough."

"You don't know anything," Arch said. He holstered his gun, and Harvey followed his example. "Get out of here, Sammy. Go home."

"I'll tell," Sammy said, like a nine-year-old.

"Go ahead, tell," Arch said. "By then it'll be too late for the old man to do anything."

"He'll kill you both."

"Not after he hears the whole story," Harvey said, "which we know and you don't."

"Aw, Arch—"

"Get out of here!"

Sammy Dolan glared at his brother for a few moments, several different expressions crossing his face—disappointment; stubborness; finally, a childish anger—then wheeled his horse around and rode back the way he had come.

"You'll be sorry," he called out, when he was almost out of sight.

"Yeah, yeah . . ." Arch said.

"Arch, what if he does tell Chance?"

"Let him tell, Ken. Like I said, it'll be too late for him to do anything about it—except maybe pat us on the back."

"And ask for his cut of the gold," Harvey pointed out.

"I don't know if I'm going to give him a cut," Arch said. "I'll have to think about that. Let's go. We got to locate those other two guards."

"How are we gonna take care of them?" Harvey asked. "If we fire our guns it will alert Adams."

"We'll worry about that when he find them," Arch said. "For now, let's just keep movin'."

As Ken rode ahead, Arch looked behind him and made sure his kid brother wasn't following them again.

At least, he hoped he wasn't.

TWENTY-THREE

Clint took the point while the guard on horseback rode drag. They were supposed to go a few miles before being picked up by the two Topeka guards.

Weatherby had not liked Clint's alterations to his plan. He thought that the two extra guards would probably be seen and would scare off the Dolan gang. . . .

"First," Clint had argued the night before he'd left for Kansas City, "there's just going to be me and the two guards, because you're not going along."

"Since when?"

"Since you don't even know if Chance has two sons or three—and what if there are other members of the gang by now?"

"And second?"

"I don't even know how these guards are going to act when push comes to shove," Clint said. "You didn't recruit any of these men personally, did you?"

"No, I didn't have time," Weatherby said. "It was either that or go to the doctor. If I hadn't gone to the doctor I'd be dead by now, or bedridden with pain."

"You see?" Clint said. "I need a little more support than you can give me."

"All right," Weatherby conceded. "But those guards better not chase Chance away."

"Let me ask you something else."

"What?"

"What if Chance isn't there? What if he just sends his boys to do the job?"

"Then I'll have to go find him, once we've taken care of his boys."

"Maybe once we have his sons he'll come to us," Clint said. "I still don't see how you can do any tracking on a horse."

"Trust me, Clint," Weatherby said, wincing at that moment from the pain, "if I need to get on a horse to get him, I will."

Clint believed in Weatherby's resolve. He just didn't believe in his physical ability anymore. . . .

Now he was on the trail with a fortune in gold, two men he didn't know anything about, and two other men who might or might not be riding along, out of sight. What if the two men from Topeka had gotten lost? What if they weren't there now, and they weren't somewhere up ahead, waiting?

Clint realized that by continually trying to do what he thought Amos Weatherby wanted—and needed—him to do he had gotten himself into a potentially deadly situation.

And he had his back to these two men.

He quickly dropped back until he was riding with the second guard, the one on horseback.

"Do you know the way to Kansas City?"

"Yes, sir."

"Why don't you take the point for a while," he suggested, "and I'll ride drag."

"Whatever you say."

Clint noticed the deep ruts the buckboard was making in the dirt. He had wondered while they were loading if the buckboard would hold, and now he wondered again. That was all they needed, for the wagon to crumple under the weight of the gold, leaving them stranded in the middle of nowhere.

He heard the two guards exchanging some words up ahead, but couldn't understand what they were saying. Maybe they were just passing the time.

He shook his head and wondered once again how he had gotten into this mess. His only way out, he decided, was to just consider himself alone—and to watch everyone.

TWENTY-FOUR

"I hate cold camps," Ken Harvey said. "I need my coffee."

"We can't risk a fire," Arch said. "Not until we've located those other two guards."

"You'd think they'd have a fire going that we could see," Harvey complained.

"They must be running a cold camp, too," Arch said. "Here, eat this." He handed Harvey a piece of beef jerky.

"Poor substitute for coffee," Harvey muttered, taking a bite.

"Stop complaining," Arch said. "When we have that gold you can have all the coffee you want—and anywhere you want it."

"Yeah," Harvey said, his eyes lighting up. "And all the women I want. What are you gonna do with your share, Arch?"

"I don't know yet," he replied. "I'm still just lookin' to pull this job off. I think that'll satisfy me even more than spendin' it."

"Not me," Harvey said. "I'm gonna enjoy bein' rich."

He bit into his beef jerky and pretended it was the finest

meal at the finest restaurant in Kansas City.

That was Ken Harvey's idea of the high life.

"You make great trail coffee, Clint," Starke said.

"Yeah, I'll have another cup," Packer said.

Clint poured each of their cups full. "When you drink your own coffee a lot, it better be good."

"Beans weren't so bad, either," Packer said. "What'd you put in them?"

"Just some bacon."

"Wish somebody knew how make it that good when we were . . ."

He got a quick look from Starke that shut him up. He had been about to say when they were riding with the Harvey gang.

"When you were what?" Clint asked.

"Riding the trail," Starke said instead.

"Who'd you ride with?"

"This outfit and that," Starke said.

"You two boys usually together?"

"Yep," Starke said.

Packer seemed to have suddenly got mute, probably because he'd almost said something he shouldn't. Clint thought it was a good idea to keep these two in front of him for the rest the trip.

Clint took the first watch, but when he woke Packer for the second he didn't get much sleep. This was not going to be an easy trip without sleep, and lugging that heavy load on the buckboard was going to add days to it. On a good horse—which he had, of course, in Duke—it was a one-day ride. With this buckboard it would probably be three.

"Wonder where them other two guards are," Packer said Clint as they changed places.

"Well, they're supposed to ride along without being seen," Clint reminded him.

"Yeah, but how do we know they're there?"

"I guess they'll let us know sooner or later," Clint said. Then he added, "Think I'll have one more cup of coffee before I turn in."

"Suit yourself," Packer said.

"So tell me," Clint said, armed with a fresh cup, "what'd you two do before you started riding security for the bank?"

"This and that."

"Not always legal, huh?"

"Well . . ." Packer looked sheepish.

"Ever been lawmen?"

"Oh, no," he said, shaking his head.

"So this must be a new experience for you."

"What?"

"Riding on this side of the law."

"Hey," Packer protested, "I never said we was ever outlaws. . . ." He looked over his shoulder, as if to make sure that Starke was still asleep.

"No, you didn't," Clint said. He finished off his coffee, tossed the remnants into the fire. "I'm gonna turn in."

"Okay," Packer said. "G'night."

"Just one thing."

"What?"

"It would be a bad idea for you and your partner to get any ideas about this gold," Clint said, "a very bad idea. Do I make myself clear?"

Packer swallowed, then said, "Yeah, real clear."

"Good," Clint said. "I'll see you in the morning." He rolled himself in his blanket, with his gun in his hand. He was still awake when Packer and Starke changed places, but it didn't look as if they had much to say to each other.

It was only when he woke up that he realized he had fallen asleep.

TWENTY-FIVE

By the middle of the next day Clint was also wondering where the guards from Topeka were. If these two had any ideas about the gold, the absence of the other two guards would certainly make them braver. And what of the Dolans? When they hit, whose side were Packer and Starke going to be on?

Clint felt like strangling Weatherby for getting him into this in the first place.

"What if there ain't no other guards?" Ken Harvey asked.

"You mean Adams lied? Why?"

"Who knows?" Harvey shrugged. "Maybe he don't trust Packer and Starke."

"Maybe he don't," Arch said, "but we can trust them, right, Ken?"

"Oh, sure, Arch," Harvey said, "they're with us. You know, we could even start a new gang. The Harvey-Dolan gang."

"The what?" Arch glared at him meaningfully.

"Okay," Harvey said, "since this job was your idea we could call it the Dolan-Harvey gang."

"That sounds good."

"Although, with Starke and Packer once riding with the original Harvey gang—"

"And you and me riding with the original Dolan gang," Arch continued, "makes us about even."

"Yeah, it does."

"Except, like you said," Arch went on, "this job was my idea."

"Okay," Harvey said, "you win. Dolan-Harvey."

"You know, we could be bigger than either of those gangs ever were," Arch said.

"Yeah, we could, starting with this job."

"And killing Weatherby."

"And killing the Gunsmith."

"We'd be notorious," Arch said.

"Legends."

"Yeah."

The two legends looked down the road and realized they'd lost sight of the wagon.

"What the—" Harvey said.

"Come on," Arch said, giving his horse his heels. "Stop daydreaming!"

Clint was now sure they were being watched from somebody riding the tree line to their right.

"Hold it!" he called out.

He rode up to the wagon, which was being driven today by Packer, while Starke rode back to join them.

"What is it?" Packer asked.

"We're being watched."

Packer started to look until Starke snapped, "Don't look around!"

Packer stopped.

"Who do you think it is?" Starke asked. "Your missing guards?"

"Maybe," Clint said.

"Or somebody else," Starke said, "somebody interested in the gold."

"Maybe."

"You're expectin' somebody, ain't you?" Starke asked.

"What makes you say that?"

"Adding those two guards," Starke said. "That's because you're waiting for someone to hit us."

Clint studied the two men for a few moments, then asked, "Have you ever heard of Chance Dolan?"

"Jesus," Packer said, "that's goin' back a ways, ain't it?"

"He's dead, ain't he?" Starke asked.

"Apparently not," Clint said.

"How do you know?" Starke asked.

"I don't," Clint said, "but Amos Weatherby does. Apparently they crossed paths three years ago."

"I heard Chance died four or five back," Packer said.

"Not if Weatherby saw him three years ago," Starke told him. Then he looked at Clint and added, "Could be he died since then, though."

"Could be, but Weatherby doesn't think so. He thinks the Dolan gang won't be able to resist this shipment."

"Who's in the Dolan gang now?" Starke asked.

"From what I heard," Clint said, "his two sons."

"Three," Packer said, "he has three . . . sons. . . ." He trailed off as he realized both men were looking at him. "What?" he said, puzzled.

"How do you know he has *three* sons?" Clint asked.

"It's just something I, uh, heard."

"You fellas are new to this game, aren't you?"

"Which game is that?" Starke asked.

"Guarding gold, or money. You're more used to stealing it, aren't you?"

"You got a big mouth, Pack," Starke muttered.

"I didn't say nothin'," Packer said, "I mean—not on purpose."

"Okay," Starke said to Clint, "so we hit a bank or two a few years ago. We been clean since then."

"And this job?"

"We didn't know what else to do," Starke said. "We didn't want to be lawmen."

"Is there any paper out on you two?"

"No," Starke said.

"So that's why the bank hired you."

"That's right. No posters, no record. We're clean."

"Well, that's good," Clint said. "You ought to stay that way, too."

"We intend to," Starke said. "If you think we took this job just to steal the gold you're wrong. On top of not wanting to steal it, we ain't ready—or stupid enough—to go up against the Gunsmith."

"I'm glad to hear that," Clint said, "but the fact of the matter is I feel sure we're being watched, and if it isn't the other two guards, then it's somebody who's waiting for their chance. We have to be ready."

"We're ready," Starke said. "Right, Pack?"

"I'm ready for anything," Packer said, patting his gun, "except like you said, going up against the Gunsmith."

"Then let's stay on our toes and be alert," Clint said. "Packer, take the point again, and let's get moving."

"Right."

Packer turned his horse and started riding.

"You're a careful man, Clint," Starke said, "keepin' us in front of you."

"I've stayed alive all these years being careful, Starke," Clint said pointedly.

"I'll remember that." Starke grabbed the reins and chirped at the team to get moving.

TWENTY-SIX

"What was that all about?" Harvey asked.

They had just watched the conversation among Packer, Starke, and Clint Adams.

"You sound worried," Arch said. "You're the one told me we could trust these two."

"We can," Harvey said. "I ain't worried about them, I'm worried about Adams. What if he caught on?"

"How could he?"

"I don't know," Harvey said. He was getting nervous the longer they went without seeing the other two guards. "If he did and he told them . . ."

"They wouldn't try anything, would they?"

"Not against him . . . and I wouldn't blame them."

"Are you sure these two rode with you pa and uncle?" Arch asked. "I thought the Harvey gang had more balls than that."

"Well," Harvey said, "they rode on two jobs, is all."

"And then what?"

"And then my pa didn't want to use them on that last job."

"How old were you?"

113

"Twenty," Harvey said. "I wanted to go, but he didn't want me, neither."

Arch wondered if old Josh Harvey knew his son would never cut it on a big job and that was why he left him behind on that last one—the one Amos Weatherby had ruined by locking everybody up.

So far Harvey had performed well when Arch and his brothers took him on jobs, but they weren't big jobs like this one. Arch had never told Sammy or Leon, but he thought their father was past the big jobs and was willing to finish out his days with small scores. Well, Arch Dolan was tired of small scores.

"Stop worrying," he said.

"When are we gonna hit them? They're already closer to Topeka than to Kansas City," Harvey pointed out.

"If those other guards don't show up, we'll let them camp and hit them at first light."

"Why not in the dark?"

"Too much chance of somebody shooting the wrong person," Arch said.

"You worried about hitting one of them?"

"No, I ain't," Arch said, "I'm worried about them hittin' one of us."

"Oh."

"But there's one other thing, Ken."

"What's that?"

"They ain't been no help at all," Arch said. "I don't want to cut them in for a share."

"They ain't gonna take kindly to that."

"That's why, first chance you get, I want you to put a bullet in Packer. I'll take Starke."

"You want to kill them, too?"

"Right after we take care of Adams. They won't be expectin' it."

"I don't know, Arch," Harvey said, shaking his head. "I invited those boys in on this."

"Hell, Ken, they weren't even real members of your pa's gang. Why should we give them a cut? Besides, how do we know they ain't plannin' the same thing? We got to hit them before they hit us."

"Well . . . maybe you're right."

"I know I'm right," Arch said. "Just think about splittin' that gold two ways."

Harvey eyes lit up as he did just that.

During the course of the day Arch Dolan figured his chances of shooting Ken Harvey after they finished killing the other three and stealing the gold.

His own eyes lit up as he thought about a one-way split.

TWENTY-SEVEN

When they camped the second night Clint decided that Weatherby was once again pulling something on him. That stubborn old man was still doing things his own way, even a few steps from his deathbed. Why else weren't those other two guards here yet?

Of course, two other things could have happened. They could have been caught and killed by the Dolan gang, or the two of them could be planning something about taking the gold. After all, there was a hell of a lot of it to go around.

Or was there?

It suddenly occurred to Clint that while he had seen the gold in the vault, he had not inspected any of the boxes. What if the gold wasn't even in the chests? What if those other two guards were off guarding the gold, wherever it really was?

What if Amos Weatherby had just flat-out lied . . . again?

Clint made sure he took the first watch again; when he was sure the two men were asleep, he went over to the buckboard. He lowered the back of the buckboard and looked at the chests. They all had locks on them. He had to figure out a way to get one open without waking up Starke and Packer.

When the chests were being loaded he'd noticed that there was a crowbar on the back of the buckboard. He didn't know if anyone else had seen it. He retrieved it now and set to work on one of the locks. If he got one of the boxes open and the gold was there, he could always come up with some kind of excuse. If the gold *wasn't* there, then he wasn't lugging these chests any farther. If the Dolan gang was up in the hills let them come down and take a look themselves. He was going to head for Topeka to wring Weatherby's skinny neck once and for all. Packer and Starke could come along and demand the rest of their money from the bank manager in Topeka.

Suddenly, he became aware of movement. He turned and saw Packer and Starke watching him. They were both wearing their guns.

"What are you doing?" Starke asked.

"Something just occurred to me."

"What?"

"That there might not be any gold in these chests."

"What?" Packer said.

"You saw the gold yourself," Starke said.

"Yes, in the vault—not in these chests."

"What makes you think there's no gold?" Starke wanted to know.

"Think about it," Clint said. "If you were the bank owners, would you send this much gold from Kansas City to Topeka with just us to guard it?"

"I wouldn't," Starke said.

"But—"

"Look," Clint interrupted Packer, "you boys might as

well know the truth. This was supposed to be a trap for the Chance Dolan gang.''

"What?"

"That's right," Clint said. "Weatherby cooked this up to nab Chance. He got me involved by telling me this gold transfer was phony."

"But it ain't."

"I'm not so sure," Clint said. "See, the bank manager in Kansas City owes him a favor. I think maybe part of paying that favor off was showing me the gold in the vault."

"You mean this is all for nothing?"

"Not for you boys," Clint said. "You got paid half in Kansas City, and you should get paid the other half in Topeka, no matter what."

"Jesus," Starke said, turning around and then turning back. "Do you hear yourself? What's what we're gettin' paid compared to what's in those chests?"

"So you *are* plannin' to try for the gold."

There was a long silence, and then Starke said, "Why don't we take a look in those chests before we declare our intentions."

"That sounds fair," Clint said, "but I think I'd prefer if one of you opened it. I don't want to have both my hands on this crowbar."

"Open it," Starke ordered Packer.

Clint handed Packer the crowbar. The guard was a bigger, younger man, and he snapped the lock in one try. He dropped the crowbar into the buckboard and opened the chest.

Arch Dolan and Ken Harvey didn't know what was going on in the camp. They simply made sure that Clint, Packer, and Starke had made camp, unhitched the horses, and started a fire before turning in themselves.

In the morning they rose, Harvey still complaining bitterly about a cold camp. They were ready to ride down on the camp and claim their prize. They moved to the vantage point from where they could see the camp and were surprised by what they saw.

"What the hell—" Harvey said.

All of the chests were off the buckboard, lying on the ground upside down, obviously empty. None of the men or the horses were in sight.

"Those double-crossers!" Arch yelled. "You said we could trust them!"

"We better get down there!"

TWENTY-EIGHT

They saddled their horses quickly and rode down into the camp. The fire was still going, but they didn't notice. They dismounted and ran to the chests.

"This one's empty," Harvey said, turning one over.

"This one, too," Arch said.

They turned over the rest and found them all empty.

"What the hell—" Harvey said again. "What do we do now? They took off with the gold."

"How?"

"What do you mean, how?"

"Think about it," Arch said. "They needed the buckboard to get this far with it. They couldn't put it in their saddlebags. How did they get away with it?"

"I don't know."

"You boys want to put your hands up?" Clint said, stepping out of hiding.

"Adams!" Arch exclaimed. "Where's my gold?"

"You mean *our* gold, don't you?" Harvey said.

"Whatever," Arch said. "I just want to know where the gold is."

"You must be a Dolan," Clint said.

"Arch."

"And you?"

"Ken Harvey."

"Harvey?"

"That's right."

"As in Josh and Jeremiah Harvey?"

"My pa and uncle."

"Never mind that," Arch said. "Where's the damn gold?"

"There is no gold," Clint said.

"You expect us to believe that?"

"Look in the back of the buckboard."

Arch walked over and did just that.

"All I see is a bunch of rocks."

"That's what was in the chests."

"But . . . why?" Harvey asked.

"This was a trap that Amos Weatherby set for you and your father."

"My pa ain't here," Arch said.

"He sent you instead?"

"He don't even know about it," Arch said. "This is my job."

"I see. You're branching out on your own."

"That's right, and I don't believe you about the gold."

"Where's Packer and Starke?" Harvey asked.

"On their way to Topeka," Clint said. "When we opened the chests last night and saw the rocks, they decided to go to Topeka and get the rest of their money from the bank for their guard duty."

"Guarding rocks!" Harvey said.

"That's right."

"Then there was no gold?" Arch asked.

"Oh, there was gold," Clint said. "I saw it in the bank."

"So where is it?"

"Well, I figure either it's still in the bank in Kansas City, or, if they were transferring it, it probably went by rail."

Arch picked up one of the rocks, hefted it in his hand, then let it drop to the ground.

"What do we do now?" Harvey asked.

"Well, for a start," Clint said, "you both drop your guns."

"Why?" Harvey demanded. "We didn't do nothin'."

"Only because there was no gold."

"You can't take us in for tryin' to steal some rocks," Arch said.

"I can take you in for a lot of other things you've done, Dolan. Once you're in custody we can work on bringing your father in."

"Forget that. You'll never catch that old man. He don't even leave home no more."

"He will when we have you."

"You got that wrong," Arch said. "He ain't gonna care."

"We'll see," Clint said. "Come on, drop 'em."

Arch and Harvey exchanged a glance but before they could act a scream ripped through the air, and then Sammy Dolan was riding into camp, his gun drawn.

"Come on, Arch!" he shouted, firing at Clint. The shot missed, and Clint didn't give him another chance. He drew and fired; his slug took Sammy Dolan right out of his saddle. He landed hard on his back in the dirt and didn't move."

"Son of a bitch!" Arch Dolan yelled, and drew his gun.

Clint turned and plugged Arch before he could get a shot off, then turned his gun on Ken Harvey.

"Don't shoot!" Harvey shouted, putting up his hands. "I give up."

"Drop your gun on the ground."

Harvey plucked his gun from his holster, dropped it, and put his hands back up.

"Now check them and make sure they're dead."

Harvey walked over to the both bodies, checked them, and announced, "They're dead, all right."

"Who was that one?" Clint asked, indicating the one who had come riding in like a wild man.

"That was Sammy."

"A Dolan?"

"Yup. The youngest."

"How many sons did Chance have?"

"Three," Harvey said. "You killed two of 'em, and he ain't gonna be real happy about that."

"I guess not," Clint said. "Who's left?"

"Leon," Harvey said. "The oldest one."

"Any other gang members?"

Harvey nodded and said, "Two, but they ain't related. Hey, were you tellin' the truth?" he asked. "About the gold, I mean?"

"Oh, yeah," Clint said. "Nothing in the chests but rocks. We can use the buckboard, though, to take those two to Topeka."

"Where's the team?"

"I've got them hidden," Clint said. "Come on, we're going to get them, and you're going to hitch them up."

"And then what?"

"And then I'm taking you all to Topeka," Clint said. "Them I'm turning over to the undertaker, and you I'm turning over to the law."

Harvey looked down at the dead body of Arch Dolan, nudged it with his foot, and said, "You and your big ideas."

TWENTY-NINE

Clint attracted a lot of attention in Topeka when he rode in beside the buckboard driven by Ken Harvey. It was obvious to everyone that there were two bodies in the back, and curiosity was always high in cases like that.

Clint directed Harvey to stop the buckboard in front of the sheriff's office. The lawman was already out front, having been alerted to what was going on.

"Sheriff," Clint said, nodding.

They had met briefly when Clint first got to Topeka. The man's name was Berry, Sheriff Wayne Berry.

"What do you have here?" Berry asked.

"This is Ken Harvey, a member of the Chance Dolan gang."

"Is that a fact? And what's in the back of the buckboard."

"As I understand it," Clint said, "I have two of Chance Dolan's sons back there, Arch and Sammy."

"You killed them?" Berry asked.

"I did," Clint said. "They didn't give me much choice, though."

"You handin' this one over to me?" Berry asked, indicating Harvey.

"I am, as well as the two dead men. They're all yours, Sheriff."

"Where are you going now?" the sheriff asked.

"I'm going to leave my horse at the livery and then go to my hotel room," Clint said. "I should be there for a couple of hours, if you need me."

"All right, Adams," Berry said. "You men. Help me here. . . ."

Clint left Sheriff Berry to his job and headed for the livery.

When the knock came at Clint's door, he figured it was either the sheriff or Amos Weatherby. He had spent a couple of hours in his room, trying to decide what to do about Weatherby. When he opened the door he saw his old friend standing there.

"What happened?" Weatherby asked.

"Why don't you come in and close the door, Amos?" Clint invited in a deceptively calm voice.

Weatherby did so, and repeated the question.

"What happened, Clint. Where's Chance?"

"Chance never showed up, Amos," Clint said, "but then why should he when there was no gold."

"I saw Packer and Starke earlier today," Weatherby said. "I can explain—"

"I don't think I want to hear it, Amos."

"The gold came in by train," Weatherby said. "I couldn't get the banks to let me use it as bait. The other guards were on the train."

"That's fine."

"You ain't mad?"

"I'm very mad, Amos," Clint said. "I'm tired of being lied to."

"Did you really bring in two of Chance's boys?"

"I did," Clint said. "They forced me to kill them."

"And how many more does he have?"

"One," Clint said, "the older one. His name is Leon. Oh, and you'll be interested in the other one I brought in. His name in Ken Harvey."

"Harvey?"

"As in Josh Harvey, his father."

"I didn't know there were any Harveys left."

"He's the last one, I guess."

"Well, this'll work, Clint," Weatherby said. "Chance is gonna come lookin' for his boys."

"That's not what Arch said when he and I talked," Clint replied. "He said his old man wouldn't care if he was in jail."

"Well, he ain't in jail," Weatherby said. "He's at the undertaker's, and that's got to make a difference."

"I guess so," Clint said, "maybe. The truth is, I don't care anymore."

"You quittin' me?"

"I'm not quitting, Amos," Clint said. "I'm just not doing this anymore."

"But we're close!"

"You get him," Clint said. "If he comes for his boys, you get him."

"But he's gonna be comin' for you, not for me," Weatherby said.

"I don't care."

"What's wrong with you?"

Clint whirled on Weatherby and said, "We said no more lies, Amos. Remember."

"You're gonna let a little lie—"

"No, not a little lie," Clint said, cutting him off. "A big lie, Amos! There was no gold in those chests. I was transporting rocks."

"I can explain that—"

"I don't want explanations," Clint said. "I don't want to hear anything you have to say anymore. I've decided that I'm out of it. You can handle the rest of this all by yourself."

"Aw, come on, lad—"

"That's it, Amos," Clint said. "I'm through."

"But . . . I need your help."

"You should have thought of that before. You should have decided to trust me, and not lie to me."

"I couldn't tell you about the gold, don't you see?" Weatherby said. "Your performance had to be perfect. If you knew—"

"Performance?" Clint repeated. "Is that what you think this all is? Some play that you're directing? And we all have no choice but to perform? Well, I've got news for you, Amos. I've got a choice."

"Clint—"

"I choose not to perform anymore."

"Aw, Clint—"

"Don't try that old man stuff with me, Amos," Clint said. "You're looking pretty healthy right now, for a man who's dying."

"I am dying!" Weatherby said. "That part wasn't a lie. Maybe the pain ain't quite as bad as I been lettin' on, but I needed you to think I was in bad—"

"Amos," Clint said, "there's the door. Use it."

"Clint . . . we're friends."

"I'm sorry you're dying, Amos," he said, "but we just aren't friends anymore. Friends don't treat each other this way."

"Clint—"

"Amos," Clint said, "get out."

Weatherby stared at Clint for a few seconds, his mouth

open and no sound coming out. He truly didn't get it, Clint thought. He didn't understand what he had done wrong.

Well, Clint wasn't making allowances anymore.

Amos Weatherby turned and left the room.

THIRTY

Clint felt bad and couldn't explain it. The man had lied to him time and again, for no good reason that he could see, so why did he feel so bad? Okay, he was dying. Maybe not as quickly as he had led Clint to believe, but that much Clint was sure of. It seemed ludicrous that even Amos Weatherby would lie about that.

Clint left his room and went downstairs. He had intended to go right to the desk and check out, and then leave Topeka, but he didn't. Instead, he went right past the desk and out onto the street. He stopped there for a moment, looking both ways, and then stepped off the boardwalk and headed for the sheriff's office.

"The editor of the *Topeka Star Herald* was already here," Sheriff Berry said. "It'll be in tomorrow's paper that Arch and Sammy Dolan, of the famous Dolan gang led by Chance Dolan, were shot and killed by Clint Adams, the famous Gunsmith."

"Great."

"The editor's gonna try to get an interview with you."

"Good luck to him. What's the paper going to say about Ken Harvey?"

"Just that he's in jail here, and that he's related to members of the Harvey gang, which was broken up five years ago by famed manhunter Amos Weatherby."

" 'Famed manhunter'?"

Berry nodded.

"The editor—his name is Lance Hunter—"

"Lance?"

Berry nodded and continued, "—was very specific about what he was going to write."

"And what's he going to say about you?"

"He's going to refer to me as a 'local lawman.' "

"Good for you."

"I'm not stupid."

"Obviously."

"Thank you."

"Has Weatherby been in to see you?"

"Yes," Berry said. "He seemed upset. What's going on?"

"I told him I wasn't going to help him anymore," Clint said.

"Can I ask why?"

Briefly, Clint explained what the situation had been between him and Weatherby over the past week or so.

"Can't say I blame you, then," Berry said. "I thought he wasn't looking very good, but I put it down to his age. Can you believe him when he says he's dying?"

"It's funny," Clint said, "but it's the one thing I do believe."

"That is funny," Berry said, "because I wouldn't believe a word he said, if I was you."

"What do you think about Chance Dolan?" Clint asked to change the subject. "Is he going to come to town looking for me?"

"I thought he was dead."

"He isn't."

"If it was me," Berry said, "I'd get out of town, but I don't have your rep."

"What if he and his gang comes to town and I'm not here? Who would he go after then?"

"Weatherby?"

"Or you."

Berry frowned. "Don't like the sound of that, much."

"See? I have to stay. I can't have him taking out his anger against me on the town."

"Are you just trying to protect Weatherby?"

Clint hesitated, then said, "Maybe."

"Well," Berry said, "if you're in a protecting mood would you keep me in mind?"

"Consider it done."

THIRTY-ONE

Before leaving the sheriff's office, Clint asked if he could talk to Ken Harvey.

"Sure, why not? The key's on the wall there."

"That's okay," Clint said. "I can do it through the bars."

Clint went into the back, where there were three cells. Only one was occupied: Ken Harvey was lying on his back on the cell cot.

"Harvey."

The man turned his head, saw Clint, and looked back at the ceiling.

"Whataya want?"

"Just to talk."

"About what?" Harvey asked. "Getting me out of here?"

"I don't think I can do that."

"Then we have nothing to talk about."

"They'll probably send you to Leavenworth, where you can see your father and uncle."

"I don't want to see them that bad."

"Well," Clint said, slowly, "maybe if you cooperate I

135

could get the sheriff to put in a word with the judge."

"Cooperate?"

"Yes."

"What kind of cooperation?"

"You could tell us where Chance Dolan and the rest of the gang is."

"That kind of cooperation could get me dead."

"Well, you could tell us if Chance is really alive. There's all these rumors that he's dead."

"He might as well be," Harvey said.

"What does that mean?"

"It means he's old, past it," Harvey said. "He's not comin' up with the big jobs anymore."

"Is that why you and Arch and Sammy went out on your own?"

"Arch and I did," Harvey said. "We was gonna be the Dolan-Harvey gang."

"What about Sammy?"

"The dumb kid tagged along," Harvey said. "He was followin' us, even after we told him to go home."

"What about the older brother? Leon? Can't he run the gang?"

"Leon is in his old man's pocket," Harvey said. "He don't make a move without Chance sayin' so."

"Is that a fact?"

"Yeah," Harvey said. "When the old man dies I don't think Leon is gonna know what to do."

"Tell me, what do you think Chance will do when he reads in the papers that two of his boys were killed by me?" Clint asked.

For the first time Ken Harvey seemed to perk up. He sat up and swung his feet to the floor.

"Is that what it's gonna say?"

"Oh, it'll mention Amos Weatherby, too."

"Weatherby," Harvey said. "You know, goin' up against you and Weatherby might get the old boy's juices goin' again."

"And if that happens he might come here."

"And he might get me out," Harvey added.

"Do you think he'll come?"

"He might."

"And how many gang members does he have left?"

"Four," Harvey answered, without thinking. "But he could get more," he added hurriedly.

"Four would be enough," Clint said. "After all, it's just me and Weatherby, and he's seventy years old."

"Same age as old Chance," Harvey said. "That'd be somethin' to see, huh? Those two old coots facin' each other in the street?"

That would be a dream come true to Weatherby, Clint thought.

"It sure would."

"Yeah," Harvey said. "Old Chance with his juices flowin' again. That'd be somethin'."

"You sure you don't want to tell us where they are?" Clint said.

"Hell, no," Harvey said. "I want Chance and Leon and the boys to come ridin' in here and take care of you and Weatherby."

"And get you out of there?"

"Damn right."

"What if after he gets you out," Clint said, "he blames you for gettin' his boys killed?"

"What? Why would he blame me?"

"Maybe he'll think that if you hadn't encouraged Arch he wouldn't be dead."

"That's stupid."

"Might even think you encouraged young Sammy."

''He wouldn't think that.''

''You don't think so?''

Harvey just stared at Clint.

''It might be something to consider,'' Clint said, ''when you're thinking about cooperating.''

Again, Harvey didn't reply.

''Just give it some thought,'' Clint said, and walked out.

THIRTY-TWO

The next thing Clint had to do was find Amos Weatherby. If he was going to stay in town and stand against Chance Dolan and his gang, then that tricky old man was going to stand with him.

He found Weatherby in the saloon they'd been in before. As he entered, the bartender waved and Clint signaled for a beer. He took it to the table where Weatherby was sitting.

The old man looked up in surprise.

"Are you forgivin' me?" he asked, hopefully.

"Hell, no," Clint said, "but I'm staying in town until we know for sure whether or not Chance is going to come after us."

"You're gonna stand with me?"

"You're going to stand with me, Amos," Clint corrected him. "After all, I'm the one who gunned down his two sons."

"I was thinkin'," Weatherby said, "about goin' to that newspaper editor and tellin' him to print that I was the one that gunned them."

"Forget that," Clint said. "I take responsibility for my own actions."

"Then what do we do?"

"One of two things," Clint said. "We wait for Chance to come after us, or we go after him."

"How do we find him?"

"I've already planted a seed with Ken Harvey," Clint said, and told Weatherby about his conversation with the man.

"You think you scared him enough?" Weatherby asked.

"I guess we'll just have to wait and see."

"Clint," Weatherby said, "I really want to apologize to you—"

"Save it, Amos," Clint said. "We're really past the stage where apologies will work. I'm only staying so that nobody else has to pay for what I did. And if I have to face Chance and his gang, you have to face them with me."

"I'll do it," Weatherby said. "You know I'll do it. That's what I wanted from the start."

"Good."

Clint noticed that Weatherby hadn't touched his beer. He wondered if the old man was feeling bad, physically.

"Amos, I need to know something for my own piece of mind, since we might be standing in the street together against four or five men."

"What?"

"I need the truth about your condition."

"I didn't lie to you about that," Weatherby said. "I'm dyin', maybe got three or four months. The pain gets bad sometimes and I take that medicine. Maybe it ain't been as bad as I made out once or twice, but it gets pretty bad sometimes."

"Like now?"

Weatherby nodded and said, "Yeah, like now. I can't even keep any liquids down."

"Then I guess tracking Chance and his gang is out of the question," Clint said. "You aren't going to be much use to me on horseback."

"You got that right."

"What about standing?" Clint asked. "Can you stand? I mean, in the street when the time comes."

"I'll stand," Weatherby said. "If I got to use my rifle as a crutch, I'll stand."

"That's not what I want you using your rifle for when the time comes, Amos, so you better make sure you can fire it."

"I'll do it," Weatherby said. "I want Chance."

"What about the money you made for this security thing? You got the gold transferred?"

"Yeah, I did."

"And you got paid."

"Yeah. You want it?"

"I don't want it. I just want to know what you're going to do with it."

"Well, I'm sending a lot of it to the doctor in San Francisco. I owe him."

"And the rest?"

Weatherby shrugged. "I'll leave it to you, if you want."

"I already told you, I don't want it."

"Then it's in the bank," Weatherby said. "I got to pay my hotel, but there's still a lot. I'll do whatever you say with it."

"I'll give it some thought," Clint said. "I should be able to think of some charity that could use it."

"Fine," Weatherby said, "whatever you say."

Weatherby's mood was so penitent that Clint couldn't help but suspect the man of something.

"It's a damn shame, Amos."

"What is?"

Clint stood up.

"There was a time I thought I could trust you," Clint said. "With anything. With my back. Now . . . I just don't know."

"You can trust me with your life, Clint," Weatherby said. "Believe me."

"I don't know that I do, Amos," Clint said, "but I guess I'm going to have to find out the hard way."

THIRTY-THREE

It took three days for one of the remaining Dolan gang to notice the piece in the Topeka newspaper. In the end, it was Leon who read it, read it again, and brought it over to where his father was sitting. He wasn't sure of his own reaction, yet. He didn't know it but he was so deep in Chance Dolan's pocket that his reaction depended on the old man's.

"Look, Pa."

"What?"

He put the newspaper on the table in front of Chance, who rarely strayed from this table in the shack they called home in Warsaw. When he got up in the morning, he sat at that table to have breakfast; at night, he got up from the table to go to sleep.

"There," Leon said, pointing.

Chance read the article, then pushed the newspaper away from him.

"So that's where they went," he said. "To hit that gold shipment on their own."

"What do we do, Pa?"

"About what?"

"Well . . . that feller Adams killed Arch and Sammy, and they got Ken in jail."

"None of that matters," Chance said. "They were fools to try it on their own. Put the three of them together you still wouldn't come up with a brain."

"So we ain't gonna do nothin'?"

Chance sat and thought a while before he answered.

"Yeah, we're gonna do somethin'," he said.

"What?"

"We're gonna make sure I don't die sittin' at this here table," Chance said. "We're gonna make sure that before I do die they'll talk about the Dolan gang again like we was somethin'."

"How we gonna do that, Pa?"

"You're gonna kill Clint Adams, boy," Chance said, "and I'm gonna kill that old fool Weatherby. I thought he was dead, anyway."

"Uh, Pa . . ."

"What?"

"I can't go up against the Gunsmith, Pa. I ain't no gunny."

"I said we was gonna kill them, you idiot," Chance said, "I didn't say it was gonna be a fair fight."

"Oh."

"Go find those other two idiots and bring them in here," Chance said. "We got plannin' to do."

"Right, Pa."

THIRTY-FOUR

Topeka became a town in waiting.

They were waiting for the circuit judge to come to town to pass judgment on Ken Harvey.

They were waiting to see if Clint Adams and Amos Weatherby were going to have a gun battle in the middle of the street with the Dolan gang.

And since word had gotten around that Weatherby was sick, they were waiting to see if he was going to die before anything could happen.

"Look at these people," Weatherby said, as he and Clint sat in front of the hotel. "They walk by and look at me like I'm some kind of freak. How did they find out, anyway?"

"My guess is the sheriff might have told that newspaper editor," Clint said.

"And who told the sheriff?"

"I did," Clint said. "I thought he deserved to know everything, since his town might end up getting shot up."

Weatherby sat silent for a few moments, then said, "Guess I can't fault you for that."

Clint had decided that he and Weatherby should stay

together most of the time—at least, when they weren't in their rooms. He didn't want either one of them getting caught in the street, facing the Dolan gang alone, and he also didn't want Weatherby keeling over and dying without him knowing it.

"They're wondering if I'm gonna get shot dead, or just fall over and die."

"I guess," Clint said. "Maybe there hasn't been much excitement in this town in a while."

"They're expectin' another O.K. Corral," Weatherby said. He looked at Clint. "I heard you was there."

"I don't want to talk about it."

"Fine," Weatherby said. "Don't talk to me. I just thought we could pass the time."

"Amos, we should stay together until the Dolans come to town, but that doesn't mean I want to talk to you. Hell, I can't believe half of what you say, anyway, so what's the point?"

"Hell, I told you I ain't gonna lie to you no more," Weatherby argued.

"And how many times have I heard that?"

"How long you gonna hold this against me, Clint?"

"I don't know, Amos. How long should I hold it against you that I had to kill two men to protect some rocks I thought was gold?"

"Hey, my job was to see to it that gold was delivered, and it was."

"You didn't have to lie to me to do it."

"Maybe not," Weatherby said, "but I did and it's over with."

"Maybe for you."

"You're acting like a woman who got cheated on."

"No," Clint said, "just a friend who got lied to."

"Why don't you just stand by and watch me face

Chance and his gang, then?'' Weatherby said. ''Watch me get gunned down? I'd take Chance with me for sure, but his son and the rest of his gang would probably get me. Then I'd be out of your hair.''

''You're not in my hair, Amos,'' Clint said, ''and you might get gunned down, but nobody will ever be able to say I stood by and watched. We're going to face that gang together, and if we live through it we'll go our separate ways.''

Weatherby frowned.

''If we live through it?''

''That's right.''

''I thought you understood from the start, Clint.''

''Understood what?''

Weatherby looked at him and said, ''I don't want to live through it.''

Clint stared at the man.

''I mean, if I live through it what do I have to look forward to? A slow death?''

Clint didn't know what to say. He wasn't going to hold back in a gun battle until Weatherby was dead. By that time he'd be dead, too.

''I'm sorry, Amos,'' Clint said, ''but I'm going to do my best to get them before they get us.''

''Your best?'' Weatherby asked. ''Hell, if there's only four of them, your best would take care of all of them. You got to promise me something, Clint.''

''What, Amos?'' Clint asked. ''What do I have to promise you?''

''Promise me you won't kill Chance,'' Weatherby said. ''That old man is mine.''

''That old man is the same age you are.''

''I know it,'' Weatherby said, ''and I'm not gonna have him outlivin' me. I won't have it!''

"Well, then, your priority is killing him, right?"

"Right, and then dyin' myself is next—dyin' in a hail of bullets, preferably."

"You sound like a dime-novel writer," Clint said.

"That's what I want when I'm gone," Weatherby said. "A dime novel about me and my last gun battle."

"Forget it, Amos."

"No," Weatherby said, "it could happen. That newspaper editor. He's a writer. Maybe he'd do it."

Weatherby got up—too fast, judging by the way he acted halfway up. He slowed down and straightened up fully.

"Where are you going?"

"To talk to that editor."

"Well, I'm staying right here," Clint said. "I can see the newspaper office from here."

"Fine," Weatherby said. "I'm sure that fella will be a lot happier to talk to me than you are."

Before Clint could answer, Weatherby stepped down from the boardwalk and started across the street.

THIRTY-FIVE

It had been a long time since Chance Dolan had been on horseback.

"We ain't never gonna get to Topeka if we have to keep stoppin'," Hal Sterling said to Dick Easy.

"Don't say that so loud," Easy said, looking over to where both Chance and Leon Dolan were sitting. "Leon might hear you. Chance had to rest, you know."

"Chance shoulda stayed behind like always and let us handle it. We could get Ken out of jail."

"I don't think Chance is worried about getting Ken out of jail," Easy said.

"Well, we can't leave him there!" Sterling said. "He's one of us."

"Chance says he stopped bein' one of us when he went off on his own with Arch and Sammy."

"Sammy didn't go with them," Sterling said. "You and me know he followed them later."

"Well, Chance doesn't care," Easy said. "He feels all three of them went off on their own and got what they deserved."

"Then why are we goin' to Topeka if not to get Ken

out, and then get back at Clint Adams for killin' Arch and Sammy?''

"Chance ain't even worried about Adams," Easy said. "It's Weatherby he wants."

"That old man?"

"He's the same age as Chance. Look," Easy said, "as long as we're part of the Dolan gang we gotta do what Chance and Leon want us to do. Me, I don't like goin' up against the Gunsmith."

"Me neither," Sterling said. "I thought Leon was supposed to handle him."

"You heard the plan," Easy said. "We got to be there anyway."

Sterling looked over to where the Dolans were sitting, and then lowered his voice.

"What if we don't want to stay part of the gang?"

Now Dick Easy looked over at the other two before lowering his voice as well.

"I was thinkin' the same thing."

"What if we just get Ken out and go our separate ways," Sterling said, "and leave Chance and Leon to deal with Adams and Weatherby."

"It'd be more of a fair fight, then," Easy said.

"It sure would."

"And we wouldn't have to worry about them comin' after us," Easy said, " 'cause Adams'll probably kill 'em both."

"Sounds like a plan to me," Sterling said.

"Hey, you two," Leon called. "Time to get goin'."

"Sure thing, Leon," Easy said, as the two men stood up. "Sure thing."

THIRTY-SIX

The sheriff stopped by and took the seat that had been vacated by Amos Weatherby.

"Where'd Weatherby go?" he asked.

"He's over at the newspaper, trying to find out if that Lance fella, the editor, wants to write a dime novel about Amos Weatherby's last showdown."

"Or last bounty."

"Whatever."

"Did you talk to Lance?"

"I haven't given newspaper interviews for a long time now," Clint said. "Nothing I ever said came out the right way."

"I know that feeling," Berry said.

"Every lawman does, I think."

"That's right, you were a lawman for a while."

"Years ago."

"Ever work with Weatherby in his prime?"

"Oh, yeah."

"He must have been somethin' to see."

"He still is," Clint said, "but in a different way."

"Yeah, I guess. Why'd you give up the law?"

"There were parts of being a lawman I couldn't deal with."

Berry laughed. "I think I know the parts you mean."

"I've got something to ask you," Clint said.

"Go ahead."

"What are you going to do when Chance Dolan gets here with his gang?"

"I'm gonna make sure they don't get my prisoner away from me."

"What about when Weatherby and I are on the street with them?"

"That's your fight, if you don't mind me sayin' so, Clint," Berry said. "I've got to look to my prisoner. I already sent a telegram to the judge telling him I had Ken Harvey in my custody. When he shows up here, I'm still going to have him."

"Can't say I blame you for that."

"I'm glad to hear it."

"And you're right," Clint said. "The rest of it is my fight, and Weatherby's."

"I got rounds to make," Berry said, standing up. "I just thought you looked like you could use some company."

"Thanks, Sheriff."

Berry hesitated, looking up and down the street.

"You figure they're just going to ride right in?" he asked.

"That's what we figure," Clint said. "I'm thinking Chance is as old as Weatherby. What's he got to lose?"

"Well," Berry said, "you did kill his sons."

"According to Ken Harvey," Clint said, "Chance won't care about that, not when he thinks they went off on their own."

"Why would he come to town, then?"

"To make a point," Clint said. "And maybe so he and Amos can settle things between them once and for all. They've got fifty years of history."

"Fifty years," Berry said, shaking his head.

"Yeah," Clint said.

The lawman waved his hand and went on about his rounds.

Lance Hunter listened to the old man who used to be Amos Weatherby ramble on about a dime novel, but all the time he was thinking about an interview with the Gunsmith.

"So what do you think, young fella?" Weatherby asked.

"Hmm? About what?" Hunter was only thirty, but he settled into a pipe the way an old man did. He regarded Weatherby over the bowl.

"About a dime novel," Weatherby said. "Ain't you been listenin'? This might be the end of an era."

Hunter wanted to be kind, so he didn't tell Weatherby that his era had come to an end a long time ago.

"I tell you what, Mr. Weatherby," Hunter said. "Do you think you can get me an interview with the Gunsmith?"

"The Gunsmith?" Weatherby asked. "I'm tellin' you about a showdown in the street between Amos Weatherby and Chance Dolan, and you want to know about the Gunsmith?"

"I'm sorry, Mr. Weatherby," Hunter said, as gently as he could, "but look at it from my point of view. You're two old men."

Weatherby stared at the young editor.

"Old men, huh?"

"I'm sorry, sir," Hunter said, "but that's the way the

public will look at it. Maybe if this had happened twenty years ago, or even ten, but now . . .''

"You know, sonny," Weatherby said, "I don't think you even know what your public wants."

"I know they'd like to read an interview with Clint Adams, the Gunsmith," Hunter said. "Can you help me with that, sir?"

"Sorry, sonny," Weatherby said, "but right now I can't even get that man to talk to me."

THIRTY-SEVEN

Clint saw the dejected set of Weatherby's shoulders as he walked back to the hotel.

"Are you in pain?" he asked as Weatherby settled back into the chair.

"No," Weatherby said, "not the kind you mean, anyway."

"Oh," Clint said. "Hunter wasn't interested?"

"Two old men," Weatherby said. "That's how he described Chance and me."

Clint didn't know what to say to that. Weatherby and Chance Dolan *were* two old men, but he couldn't very well say that.

"I know what you're thinkin'," Weatherby said.

"What?"

"That we are two old men."

Clint didn't respond.

"You know what that young pup editor wanted from me?" Weatherby asked.

"What?"

"He wanted me to arrange an interview with you. All he wanted to talk about was the Gunsmith."

Again, Clint was stuck for something to say—but since he really didn't want to talk to Amos Weatherby, that wasn't a bad thing.

"You know, it's funny," Weatherby continued. "All these years I've heard that name, 'the Gunsmith,' and I knew it was you, but to me you were always just Clint, you know? I guess it never dawned on me that you were a legend."

"I'm no legend."

"You are to the public," the older man said. "I'm an old man, but you're a legend, and that's what they want."

Weatherby looked up and down the street.

"Look at the street," he said. "It's empty."

"So?"

"Everybody knows what's comin'," Weatherby said. "They're all behind closed doors, but they'll be at their windows, ready to watch when the time comes—but they won't be watching Amos Weatherby facing Chance Dolan. No, they'll be watching the Gunsmith face the Dolan gang. That's the way it'll get written up."

"Amos, are you jealous?" Clint asked.

Weatherby looked at him and said, "Maybe . . . maybe envious."

"Don't envy me, Amos."

"I envy your youth. I guess I envy the respect you command."

"You command respect."

"No," Weatherby said. "I did once, but not anymore, not as an old man. You'll find out, Clint—or maybe you won't. I don't know. When you're my age I guess you'll still be 'the Gunsmith.' "

"I wish you'd stop saying that."

"Why? Don't you like it?"

"To tell you the truth, no," Clint said. "It's not something I call myself."

"It's what everybody calls you," Weatherby said, "so it's who you are."

"See," Clint said, "I don't believe that. You're not an old man, Amos, just because people call you one."

"I'm an old man because I'm old," Weatherby said.

"And I'm Clint Adams because that's who I see when I look in the mirror. Not some legend built up in the minds of the public or on the pages of a newspaper or dime novel."

"There's another thing."

"What?"

"Dime novels," Weatherby said. "You've had them written about you. You, Hickok, Masterson, Earp, your whole generation. Chance and me, what are we gonna have?"

"You're getting ready to put on a show," Clint said, "only you're figuring nobody is going to show up."

"Oh, they're gonna show up, all right," Weatherby said. "But to see you, not to see me and Chance."

"Maybe," Clint said, "if you tell Chance that, you and him can just walk away from this."

"And where does that leave me?" Weatherby asked. "Still dyin' in bed. I don't want that. I'd rather die in the street with everyone watchin' and nobody carin'."

Clint was thinking his old friend just might get his wish.

THIRTY-EIGHT

Sometime later Sheriff Berry came walking back over to where Clint and Weatherby were sitting.

"What's on your mind, Sheriff?" Clint asked.

"It's not what's on my mind," Berry said. "It's my prisoner."

"What about him?" Clint asked.

"He says he wants to talk to you, Adams."

"Me? About what?"

"He won't tell me," Berry said. "He'll only tell you."

Clint looked at Weatherby.

"You go ahead. I'll keep watch here."

"You'll call me as soon as you see anything?"

"I'll sing out loud and clear."

Clint turned to the lawman and said, "Okay, then, let's go."

He followed Sheriff Berry back to the jail, and the lawman left him alone with Ken Harvey.

"What do you want?" Clint asked.

"I wanna cooperate."

"It's a little late for that."

"No, it ain't," Harvey said. "I can tell you where Chance's hideout is."

159

"He won't be there," Clint said. "More than likely he's on his way here."

"I told you," Harvey said, "Chance ain't gonna want no revenge for Arch and Sammy."

"Chance is going to want Amos Weatherby," Clint said. "That's what's going to bring him here."

"I can tell you, anyway," Harvey said. "You can pass it on to the law in Missouri. Maybe they'll find some of Chance's stuff."

"His stuff?"

"Things he's stole."

"Like what? Money? My bet is Chance spent the money he stole just as fast as he could all his life."

"This ain't fair," Harvey said. "You said you'd talk to the judge."

"I said I'd talk to the sheriff and he'd talk to the judge," Clint said, "*if* you cooperated."

"That's what I wanna do," Harvey argued. "Cooperate!"

"It's too late now, Harvey."

"No, it ain't," the outlaw insisted. "Look, go to Warsaw."

"Warsaw? Where's that?"

"It's a little town in Missouri. Chance has a shack just outside of town. That's where he holes up after a job."

"I think you're shit out of luck, Harvey," Clint said. "My bet is that if Chance and his boys come out on top the next thing they'll do is bust you out of here—"

"Yeah!"

"—to kill you."

"What? I didn't do nothin'?"

"You followed Arch, didn't you?" Clint asked. "You turned your back on Chance. I'll bet he won't forget that."

"Adams," Harvey said, "you gotta get me out of here!"

"I can't do that, Harvey," Clint said. "You'll have to take that up with the sheriff. You're his prisoner."

"But you brung me in."

"It don't matter who brings you, Harvey," Clint said, on his way out, "it's who's got you now."

On his way out Clint said to Berry, "I think he'll talk to you now, sheriff."

"About what?"

"Just about anything you like, I'll bet."

THIRTY-NINE

When they drew near Topeka, Chance Dolan called their progress to a halt again and dismounted unsteadily.

"Another rest stop?" Sterling said to Easy. "We're almost there."

"Shhh," Easy said, but it was too late; Leon had heard.

"You got a problem, Sterling?" he growled.

"No, Leon, no problem," Sterling said quickly. "I was, uh, just wonderin' why we're stoppin' so close to town, is all."

"Pa wants to go over everythin' so there's no mistake," Leon said.

"Gather round here, boys," Chance called out.

Leon gave both Sterling and Easy a hard look; they dismounted and joined him in walking over to where Chance was sitting on a rock.

"We're gonna be ridin' into Topeka in a little while," Chance said. "They might be expectin' us."

"Why?" Easy asked.

"Because they have one of us in their jail," Chance said. "They might be expectin' us to come in and try to get him out."

"Then should we go in separately?" Sterling asked.

"No," Chance said, "we're goin' in together, and we're ridin' right down the center of the main street."

"Uh, is that wise, Chance?" Sterling stammered. "I mean, if they're waitin' for us—"

"If somebody's waitin' for us," Chance said, "it's Adams and Weatherby."

"Two against four?" Sterling said. "That doesn't sound so bad."

"You three will take care of Clint Adams," Chance said. "Amos Weatherby is mine. That old man has had this comin' to him for a long time."

"Can you take him, Pa?" Leon asked.

"Weatherby knows that I've always been faster than him," Chance said.

Leon frowned. He remembered the time in Kansas City three years ago when he and Arch had stood with Chance against Weatherby. In that saloon, both Chance and Weatherby had agreed that the old manhunter was faster, but Chance was smarter. Why, three years later, did Chance suddenly think he was the faster, and always had been?

"Pa."

"What is it, Leon?" Chance asked.

Leon looked at Sterling and Easy, and decided not to question his father in front of them.

"Do you think the local law will side with them?" he asked instead.

"I think the local law will stand by and watch, Leon," Chance said. "This is between us and them. Besides, the sheriff is gonna have to keep an eye on the jail."

"What do we do, after it's all over? Do we get Ken out of jail?" Easy asked.

"We get him out, all right," Chance said, "so I can kill him."

"What?" Sterling asked. "What for?"

"For bein' disloyal," Chance said. "He went off with Arch and Sammy, didn't he? They all deserved to die for that. Harvey got a break and lived. I'm gonna make sure he don't live too long."

"Chance . . . he's one of us," Easy protested.

"Not anymore," Chance said. "Now, let's mount up and go take care of this."

As they mounted up, Leon decided to let Sterling and Easy take care of Clint Adams while he backed his father up against Weatherby. He just didn't think his father was thinking right, at the moment.

They mounted up and started the last part of the ride to Topeka.

Easy and Sterling lagged behind so they could talk.

"Do you think the three of us can take the Gunsmith?" Sterling asked.

"I don't know," Easy said, "but I don't aim to find out."

"What should we do?"

"I think we should get Ken out of jail, and the three of us should get the hell outta here."

"Chance'll be after us, then," Sterling said, "for sure."

"Chance can't come after us," Easy said. "He can hardly sit his horse. Besides, after today he'll probably be in jail or dead."

"So what about Leon?" Sterling asked. "He'll come after us?"

"The three of us can handle Leon," Dick Easy said. "All we got to do is stick together."

Sterling bit his lip.

"Are you with me?" Easy asked.

Sterling thought about it a little longer, then finally nodded and said, "Yeah, okay, I'm with you."

"Just watch for my signal," Easy said. "When the action starts, we'll make our move."

FORTY

When Clint got back to the hotel Amos Weatherby was sitting in the chair with his eyes closed. Clint stopped and stared at him. He could not detect the rise and fall of the man's chest. He continued to stare, wondering if Weatherby had simply died in that chair, when suddenly the old man's eyes opened. In that moment Weatherby looked even more ancient than his seventy years. Clint noticed that his eyes were runny and unfocused.

"Did you think I was dead?"

"The thought crossed my mind," Clint confessed.

"Or did you hope?"

"Why would I do that? I don't wish you dead, Amos."

"That's good to know."

Weatherby used the thumb and middle finger of his right hand to clear the fluid from his eyes.

"You know," he said, "lately I been thinkin' that there are worse things than dyin'."

"Is that a fact?" Clint asked. He was staring off down the street, where four riders had appeared. They were riding slowly.

"Like what?"

167

"Like gettin' old," Weatherby said. "Everything hurts, nothin' works right, you got fluid comin' from your eyes and nose and other parts of your body that you got no control over."

"Sounds to me like you're right, Amos," Clint said. "There are worse things than dying."

"What are you lookin' at?" Weatherby asked.

"Riders."

"How many?"

"Four."

"Comin' fast?"

Clint shook his head.

"Slow."

"Recognized anyone?"

Clint looked at Weatherby.

"Why would I?"

Weatherby got up—slowly, Clint noticed—and moved to a point where he could also look up the street.

"I see 'em," he said.

"Recognize anyone?"

"Not from here, I don't," Weatherby said. "Not with these eyes. We'll just have to wait for them to come closer."

Riding down the street, Chance was struck by how empty it was.

"They're expectin' us, all right," he said to Leon.

"They're all hidin'."

"Not all of them."

They could both see down the street to where one man was standing, watching them.

"Know him?" Leon asked.

"Can't tell from here," Chance said. "Not with these eyes."

This was the first reference Leon had ever heard his father make to age.

Suddenly, a second man appeared to stand next to the first.

"Him?" Leon asked.

"Can't see from here, dammit!" Chance said. "I told you that."

"Pa—"

"You've seen Weatherby," Chance said. "Three years ago, in Kansas City."

"Mostly from the back," Leon said.

"Fine," Chance said, "then we'll just have to wait until we get a little closer."

FORTY-ONE

Suddenly, Amos Weatherby started to laugh.

"What's so funny?" Clint asked.

"We are," Weatherby said, then clarified the statement by adding, "Chance and me. I'll bet neither one of us can recognize the other because of our eyes. We're both waiting until we get closer together."

"That's funny?"

"Sure, it is," Weatherby said. "I even wonder if we'll be able to hit each other when we start shootin'."

"You two have know each other a good long time," Clint said.

"A *good* long time," Weatherby said.

"How long?"

"When we first met," Weatherby said, "we was courtin' the same red-haired girl. We was sixteen and she was fourteen."

"What happened to her?"

"She didn't go with either one of us," Weatherby said. "She picked somebody else."

"So you're from Missouri, then?"

"That's right."

"I didn't know that," Clint said, surprised. "Were you ever friends?"

"Once," Weatherby said, "before that red-haired gal."

"But she didn't pick either one of you."

"Didn't matter," Weatherby said. "We knew then that we'd probably always want the same things. Can't be friends when that's the case."

Clint couldn't think of an argument for that.

"So it's more than fifty years that you know each other."

"When you get to fifty years you stop countin'."

"What if you could be friends again?"

"Too much water under the bridge," Weatherby said. "Besides, I spent my life upholdin' the law and he spent his breakin' it. Somethin's gotta give, don't you think?"

"I guess . . ."

"I can't even tell if that's him by the way he sits his horse," Weatherby said. "Well, one of them fellas sits his horse like an old man, so maybe it is him."

"Maybe we should step out into the street," Clint said, mostly kidding, "and if it's Chance and his men they'll start shooting at us."

"That's a sound idea," Weatherby said, and he stepped forward before Clint could stop him.

FORTY-TWO

"That's got to be Weatherby," Chance said.

"Why?" Leon asked.

"Look at him, he moves like an old man. Besides, no one else would be stupid enough to step into the street like that."

At that moment the other man followed Weatherby into the street.

"Well," Leon said, "almost no one else . . ."

"Amos, what the hell are you doing?" Clint demanded, moving alongside the older man.

"Getting this over with, whataya think? Don't stand too close to me, Clint. Don't you remember anything I taught you?"

"I remember everything," Clint muttered, "I just don't know how much of what I remember is true."

Weatherby rolled his eyes. Death would be a relief, just to get away from Clint's whining. What the hell was a little lie between friends?

Behind the two Dolans, Sterling and Dick Easy were still waiting to make their move.

"When do we get away?" Sterling asked.

"When the shooting starts," Easy said.

"Hey, wait," Sterling said. "What happens if *we* get shot?"

"Just move when I do," Easy said, "and you won't get shot."

The sheriff's office came into view just about the time the two men's faces did. Easy just hoped that Chance would stop near it. . . .

"Okay," Chance said, reining in his horse.

"Okay—what?" Leon asked.

"That's Weatherby."

"And the other man is the Gunsmith?"

"I don't know," Chance said. "I only remember Weatherby."

He made a move to dismount, but felt a pain in his lower back.

"Leon," he said bitterly, "help me off this damned horse!"

"Jesus," Weatherby said.

"What?"

"Look. He needs help gettin' off his horse."

"Is that him?"

"Of course it's him," Weatherby said, "but look how old he looks."

Clint didn't say anything, but to him Chance Dolan looked just like Amos Weatherby.

When Chance Dolan was on the ground Leon said, "Pa, look."

"What?"

"We're right near the sheriff's office."

Chance ignored it.

"He's not gonna take a hand," he said confidently. "It's between us and them, me and Amos."

"And Adams?"

"I told you," Chance said. "He's all yours. I just want Amos."

Chance and Leon both turned to face Clint and Weatherby. Sterling and Easy stood behind the two Dolans uneasily.

"Pa . . ." Leon said. Something occurred to him as he stared at Amos Weatherby.

"What is it?"

"It's Weatherby, Pa," Leon said.

"What about him?"

"Well . . . I didn't get a good look at him three years ago in that saloon in Kansas City . . ."

"So?"

"So I'm gettin' a good look at him now."

"Well, that's good, boy," Chance said. "I'm glad you can see him, 'cause you're gonna see him die."

"But, Pa . . ."

"What is it?" Chance repeated testily.

"He—he looks just like you."

Clint suddenly got an uneasy feeling.

"Amos."

"What?"

"There's one more lie in there, isn't there?"

Weatherby hesitated, then said, "It ain't a lie, exactly."

"Then what is it?"

"More like . . . whataya call it, when you leave somethin' out?"

"Omission?"

"Yeah, right," Weatherby said. "It's just an omission."

"And what did you omit, Amos?" Clint asked. "That Chance looks just like you?"

"Yeah, yeah," Weatherby said, "he should look just like me. . . . He's my twin brother."

FORTY-THREE

"That's a hell of a big omission!" Clint snapped.

"What the hell is the difference to you?"

"You know," Clint said, "I'm not exactly sure why, but it does make a difference—and big one."

"Amos!" Chance Dolan called out.

"Hello, Chance."

"Had to come to this, didn't it?"

"I guess so."

"Hey, wait a minute!" Clint said, stepping forward.

"What are you doin'?" Weatherby snapped.

"What's your name, son?" Clint asked the young man next to Chance. He looked enough like him to be his son. "Are you Leon, the oldest boy?"

"That's right."

"Leon, don't you notice something strange about these two?"

"Well . . . I did notice somethin' just now . . ."

"Like how alike they look?"

"Well . . . yeah." Leon had a confused look on his face.

"There's a good reason for that, Leon," Clint said,

"and I just found this out myself. They're brothers."

"What?"

"In fact, according to Amos here, they're twin brothers."

Leon turned his confused look on his father.

"Pa?"

"So we're brothers, so what?" Chance asked.

"But . . . how? Why?" Leon asked. "Why didn't you ever tell us?"

"It wasn't none of your business."

"The same goes for you, Clint," Amos said.

"No, I think it *is* our business, Leon's and mine. He and I stand to get killed here, and over what? What's this all about, anyway?"

Neither Weatherby nor Chance replied.

"I think I know," Clint said, suddenly. "By God, it's that girl, isn't it? This has been going on for over fifty years because of a girl?"

"Not just a girl," Chance said.

"An angel," Weatherby said.

"And he took her from me," Chance said.

"Like hell," Weatherby said. "You took her from me."

"If Amos told me the truth," Clint said, rolling his eyes at the prospect, "she didn't go with either of you."

"And that was his fault, too," Chance said.

"No it wasn't, it was yours!" Weatherby said.

"You see?" Clint said to Leon. "We're going to take a chance on getting killed because they're still fighting over a girl fifty years later."

Leon frowned, thought a moment, then said, "That's stupid."

"Yes, it is," Clint said, "and I, for one, am not going to do it."

"What are you talkin' about?" Weatherby asked.

"I'm stepping out of this, Amos," Clint said. "This is between you and your brother."

"What?"

"What about you, Leon?" Clint asked.

"But . . . you killed my brothers."

"Does your father care about that?" Clint asked. "They were his sons. Does he care? Does he care about you? He's willing to get you killed right here and now, isn't he?"

"Pa?"

"Your brothers were stupid and disloyal, Leon. Don't you be, too," Chance said.

Leon looked at Clint, who shrugged.

"I'm out, Pa," Leon said. He looked behind him and saw that Sterling and Easy had already taken off. "And the boys are gone."

Clint walked over to one side of the street, the side the sheriff's office was on, and stepped up onto the board-walk.

"It's stupid, Pa," Leon said. "Stupid to fight over a woman this long."

Leon walked to the other side of the street.

"You two can kill each other if you want," Clint said. "You let this feud push you onto opposite sides of the law all these years, it might as well end this way."

"That's fine with me," Chance said.

"Me, too," Weatherby said, and they both went for their guns, surprising Clint, who thought he could talk them out of it.

He couldn't.

It had been a long time since either man had tried to draw his gun quickly. Neither had the dexterity for it. Weatherby's gun came out of his holster and kept going. He made a grab for it as it flew into the air, but he missed, and it landed in the dirt.

Chance Dolan's hand cramped as soon as he tried to draw his gun, and it simply fell from his limp fingers.

Both men stared at each other, and then down at their guns.

"If either one of you tries to pick 'up your gun," Clint said, "you'll break something."

Both men looked at Clint, eyes thick with liquid.

"It's over," Clint said.

He stepped into the street, picked up Chance's gun first, and then Weatherby's. Then he waved Leon over.

"Take your father home, Leon," Clint said. "Your brothers are dead, and your gang looks broken up. Find something else to do."

"Yes, sir," Leon said. "Come on, Pa."

Chance looked at Weatherby and said, "Amos."

"Chance," Weatherby replied.

Leon boosted Chance Dolan up onto his horse, then mounted his own. Chance was still holding his cramped hand to his chest, so Leon took the reins of his horse and led him back the way they had come, out of town.

Clint looked at Weatherby and said, "You're a stupid old man."

"If I'm so stupid," Weatherby said, "how come I notice those other two men's horses are still here?"

Clint looked over at the horse, and then back at Weatherby.

"The jail," he said, and handed Amos Weatherby back his gun.

FORTY-FOUR

When Clint and Weatherby entered the jail they found Sheriff Berry on the floor, bleeding from a gash on his head. Ken Harvey was gone.

Clint ran to the sheriff and bent over him. He was relieved when the man's eyes fluttered open.

"Back door," Berry said, "back door . . ."

"Stay with him!" Clint called to Weatherby. He went out the back, figuring the three men would head for the livery stable. They wouldn't chance doubling back around to the front of the building—or would they? Could they be that dumb?

He was running up the alley next to the jail to the street when he heard the shots.

Obviously, Weatherby had not stayed with the sheriff.

As soon as Clint went out the back door, Weatherby leaned over the sheriff and said, "Are you all right?"

"I'm fine," Berry said. "Go!"

Well, Clint had told him to stay, but the law was telling him to go, and he was always one to obey the law.

He ran out the front door, gun held firmly in his hand.

As he burst out onto the boardwalk he saw the three out-laws trying to mount two horses.

"Hold it!" he shouted.

Sterling was sitting his horse alone while Dick Easy was trying to lift Ken Harvey onto the back of his. When he heard Weatherby's voice, he aimed his gun at the old lawman and fired. At the same time, Weatherby raised his gun and fired. He was aiming at Sterling, but hit Easy in the shoulder, knocking him off his horse. He felt something tug at his sleeve as he watched Ken Harvey fall to the ground, also.

Clint came running out of the alley as Sterling was steadying his horse for another shot at Weatherby. Clint drew and fired, blasting the outlaw from his horse.

Weatherby ran forward and pointed his gun at the fallen Harvey.

"Hold it!" he said.

"Don't shoot!" Harvey said. "I ain't armed."

Clint rushed up next to Weatherby and said, "Amos, damn it!"

"Had to do it, Clint," Weatherby said. "The sheriff told me to."

Clint looked at Weatherby's arm and said, "You're hit."

"Just a scratch," Weatherby said. "Another scratch in a long line of 'em."

"Well, you're lucky it wasn't your last."

Weatherby shook his head and said, "I ain't so sure about that, Clint."

After they got Harvey back into his cell, a doctor came by to look at both the sheriff and Weatherby. The saw-bones bandaged them both, pronouncing them fit.

"Scratches, mostly," he said, "although the sheriff bled a lot. They'll both be fine."

"Thanks, Doc," Clint said.

"They could both use some rest," the doc said. "Your friend looks worse than he should, but then at his age . . ."

"I know, Doc," Clint said, "I know."

After the doc left, Clint told Weatherby to go back to the hotel and get some rest.

"It's all over, Amos," Clint said.

"Chance is still out there."

"What does it matter?" Clint asked. "In the grand scheme of things, what does it matter."

Clint arose the next morning, ready to leave Topeka. Whatever Weatherby decided to do, he was done. That last lie had been one too many. Imagine battling your own brother for fifty years because of a woman—a girl, really, from their childhood. Two young fools who grew into old ones.

He left his room and walked down the hall to Weatherby's. He knocked, but there was no answer. Either he was sound asleep, or he'd already gone downstairs.

"Amos?" Clint knocked again, but there was no answer. He had a key to the room, so he used it.

Weatherby was lying in bed, on his back, his eyes closed. He looked like he was sleeping peacefully, but Clint needed only one look to know the truth. Sometime during the night his old friend's heart had finally stopped.

"Now it really is all over, Amos."

Part of the way back to Missouri Leon decided they should camp for the night so Chance could rest. In the morning he went to wake his father, but he couldn't. Time had run out for the old man. He buried him right there, then sat by the grave for a while, wondering what he should do with his life. He had no father, no brothers, no friends.

But at least he had time.

Watch for

DEATH TIMES FIVE

209th novel in the exciting GUNSMITH series
from Jove

Coming in June!